THE PRICE OF PASSION

THE PRICE OF PASSION

The Legacy Series – Book Four

by

Vicki Hopkins

HOLLAND
LEGACY PUBLISHING

DEDICATION

To my wonderful readers who found this series worth following. Thank you for allowing me to entertain you with a story of innocence, deception, love, and passion. Remember that everything carries a price.

TABLE OF CONTENTS

PROLOGUE

Alastair locked the door to his bedroom suite and dashed across to the other side. In a frenzied motion, he grabbed the handle to his closet, flung it open, and reached to the shelf above his head. Red-faced and burning with anger, he searched for the box. Unable to find it, he frantically tossed his belongings to the floor. At last the wooden case emerged, and Alastair snatched it from its hiding place.

His heart pounded heatedly as he held the custom walnut case and considered the contents. Some time ago he purchased the item for display but never felt inclined to carry a weapon—at least not until today. He rubbed his hand along the wood grain and wiped away the dust. Inside lay a 1908 vest pocket Colt automatic pistol, which was more than adequate to do the job.

Walking over to his writing table, he sat down and opened the lid. The casing of metal gun shimmered from the streaming light of his desk lamp. Alastair carefully pulled out the nickel-plated firearm by the ivory grip. His hand shook as he fingered the trigger. It would only take one shot to end the sordid affair.

He laid the gun on the tabletop and examined the contents of the box. It contained the manufacturer's cleaning tools, an empty magazine, and fifty-four .25-caliber bullets placed point down in round holes. The interior lid of the case included written instructions. Alastair briefly scanned the document until he felt confident in handling the weapon.

Picking up the magazine, he opened the metal closure and then methodically removed six bullets. One by one he placed them in the metal container and then closed it shut. With force, he shoved it into the bottom grip of the gun and pushed it upward until it clicked. The firearm, no bigger than the palm of his hand, lay on his cold flesh, loaded and ready to hit its target.

He jolted when hearing a loud pounding on his door.

"Alastair, let me in!"

"Go away, Grace," he growled. "I have nothing to say." After three more pounds of his sister's fist, she bellowed again.

"Let me in before you do something rash," she howled.

"Rash?" He rose from his chair and strode with heavy footsteps toward the door. In his right hand he clutched the loaded gun. "Do you think we should stand by and do nothing after what *he* has done to her?" His body trembled as he screamed his livid response.

"Alastair, let me in," Grace moaned, lowering her voice in a tearful plea.

With his chest constricting in rage, he knew he had to shut her up or she would awaken the entire household. Her pounding heightened his agitated state.

With his cold left hand, Alastair reached forward and turned the metal doorknob. Grace, surprised at his surrender, stood stiffly on the other side of the threshold. Her reddened face matched the color of her lipstick. When she glanced at his stance and noticed the gun clutched in his right hand, she gasped aloud.

"What are you doing with that gun?"

"It's none of your business," he barked. Alastair's eyes grew dark. His soul hardened with disdain. He'd never felt such an urge to stop a wicked, beating heart in the chest of a man as he did at that moment. Besides, without her, his life held no value. The gallows would be sufficient to ease his emotional pain and well worth the spectacle of watching a blackguard die at his feet.

"Where are you going?" Grace pitched forward and grabbed his arm.

"Out of my way," he demanded with clenched teeth. In a quick jerk he pulled free of her grasp and headed for the door.

"No, Alastair! Don't do this!"

He would hear none of her pleas. Swiftly he ran down the stairs and heard the frantic footsteps of Grace follow closely behind. As he reached the front entrance and swung the door open, she clutched his arm tightly with both hands, digging her nails into the sleeve of his coat.

"I beg of you, don't do something you'll regret," she cried. Frightful tears moistened her eyes.

Alastair gazed into his sister's horrified countenance. "Let me go, Grace, before I am forced to hurt you." It deeply pained his heart having to threaten her, but she needed to stop and leave him to carry out his intent.

Astonished at his words, she quickly released him and stepped backward. Grace brought her hands to her mouth, trembling over his threat. Alastair said nothing more and walked into the night, hell-bent on killing the vilest human being on earth.

CHAPTER 1

Robert Holland sat leisurely in the wingback chair, looking confident and at ease. One arm dangled over the side of the armrest while the other held a glass of Irish whiskey.

"Let me get this straight," Alastair said, glancing at his friend with suspicion. "You want me to approve your intentions to court my sister Grace."

"Yes, that is my request."

"And why on earth would I agree to let you play with her affections? You realize that I am acquainted with your reputation with the female population."

"Because, ole friend, I am a changed man." Robert smirked.

Alastair took a sip of his brandy and somberly stared at Robert. His longtime friend appeared too self-assured for his taste. He wanted to see him squirm like a worm in his new business attire. It would be a clever ploy to drag the conversation out a bit longer before giving his reluctant consent.

For years he'd watched Robert pursue mindless and morally loose women for entertainment. It concerned Alastair that he had no real knowledge of how many he had bedded behind closed doors. Perhaps his actions had been merely for show to look superior to his cousin Geoffrey. Maybe underneath that blond head of hair and behind those blue eyes existed a moral and honest man.

Alastair thoughtfully stroked his chin. No, he could not

believe that Holland changed to such an extent or had not visited the underskirts of a few women recently. Truth be told, Alastair wrestled with his male urges, being the same age as Robert. The two of them were no different. Regrettably, the nagging question remained—would his friend respect his sister? He leaned forward and gazed into Robert's determined gaze, looking for a hint of falsehood.

"Why the sudden interest in Grace? For years you have not given my sister anything more than a mere glance or acknowledgment of her existence. Now you declare that you wish to pursue her affections." He paused and frowned. "You must possess ulterior motives, and I will not allow you to ruin her reputation." Alastair deepened his voice to accentuate the warning.

Robert sighed and shifted in his seat. Apparently his assured confidence began to wane during his interrogation. The glass of whiskey that Alastair offered him earlier retained a small amount. Robert took the last sip and set the crystal on a side table.

"I promised Jolene over a year ago that I would consider drawing closer to Grace, but life has kept me occupied with career matters. You know very well how much time I have spent these past eight months getting settled at the law firm." Robert's tone rose slightly, displaying his exasperation. "The demands of the business are grueling, to say the least."

"True," Alastair said, nodding his head. "I will admit you barely have time for our friendship." He gulped his last bit of brandy and set it down next to Robert's empty glass. "What exactly attracts you to Grace that you suddenly find her of interest?" he inquired with a wary frown.

Robert cleared his throat and lowered his head. "Well, she is quite attractive." He grinned mischievously. "Not to mention well-mannered, accomplished, and from a good family," his smooth voice boasted. "And from what I have heard from acquaintances, she has nurtured a silent crush on me for some time."

"Ha!" Alastair roared. "Who told you, Jolene?"

"Well, she hinted that I should consider Grace because of her personality, but I surmised as much because of the way Grace regards me from afar and when we are near." Robert paused. "You know that a man can tell when a lady has eyes for him."

"You are a damn rogue, Holland, and I don't trust you." Alastair's brow wrinkled, half in doubt and anger. He was about to continue his rant when the door to the parlor flew open. Grace bounced across the threshold with a book in her hand. Her steps came to an abrupt halt when she saw Robert lounging in a chair next to Alastair on the divan.

"Oh," she said, raising her brow in surprise. "I apologize for intruding. No one told me that we had company." She glanced over at Robert and attempted to restrain a smile.

Alastair and Robert rose to their feet in unison to acknowledge her presence. "Well, since you arrived at an opportune time, why don't you sit with us awhile?" He motioned to the seat next to him.

"I don't wish to intrude," she said. "But if you insist."

Grace sauntered over to the divan and sat down, and the men returned to their seats. Robert eyed her before offering a compliment.

"You look well this afternoon. Is that a new dress? I don't recall seeing that particular pattern in your wardrobe before."

Alastair noted a distinct twinkle in Robert's eyes as he inspected his sister's new frock. The scoundrel already began his wiles of flattery.

"Thank you," Grace replied. "It is new." She paused and gazed at him suspiciously. "However, I am a bit surprised, Robert, you even noticed. I don't recall you expressing approval of my attire in the past," she pointed out.

Alastair chuckled approvingly at her guarded reply.

"I have been neglectful indeed," Robert replied. He sounded sickly sweet while justifying his newfangled attentiveness.

"So," Grace said cheerily, "what brings you to our humble home? Are you and Alastair planning future engagements with lady friends?" Grace quizzically glanced back and forth at them.

Alastair sniggered and then cleared his throat. "You could say that," he replied. His eyes shifted over to Robert, deciding to put him on the spot. "A few minutes ago Robert asked me for my permission to court you. What do you think, Grace? Shall I let him?"

Grace gasped and dropped the book clutched in her hand. It landed with a thud at her feet, and a rosy blush flushed her cheeks. Robert played the hero and picked it up, handing it back to her with a smile.

"I-I-" Grace stuttered, falling into a momentary silence. After regaining her composure, she continued. "Suddenly I'm at a loss for words." Her eyes sparkled, and a flirtatious smile curled her lips.

"Would you do the honor of having dinner with me tomorrow evening?" A broad grin spread across Robert's face.

"Now wait a minute," Alastair interjected, annoyed. "I have not agreed to this arrangement yet."

"Oh, Alastair, why does he need your permission?" Grace chided. "You are not Father." She flashed an irritated glare.

"I doubt Father will be pleased either. He is acquainted with Robert's reputation with the ladies," he countered.

Robert pursed his lips and returned an exasperated glance at Alastair. "I asked you because of my respect for you as my friend. It's only fair to acknowledge my intentions regarding your sister." In a surprise move, Robert leaned forward and grabbed Grace's hand and held it tight.

"So say yes, Miss Whitefield, that you will dine with me tomorrow evening."

Grace smiled demurely and lowered her eyes. A flush of shyness continued to tint her cheeks.

"You know that I will, Robert. I can think of nothing else I would rather do."

"Oh, for heaven's sake, Grace," Alastair roared. "You could put him off a bit. Do not be so eager. Make him suffer for a few minutes at least." He snickered. "I want to see him squirm."

"There," Robert announced loudly. "It is settled." He released Grace's hand. "Your sister has consented, and there is nothing that you can do about it."

"Well, there bloody well is," Alastair shot back. "I have terms, Holland."

"Terms?" Robert sat up straight. "What do you mean?" he inquired with agitation in his voice.

"I nurture intentions toward your half sister Jolene. As Grace is well aware, I have not stopped thinking about her since the day we met. It is my intention to begin corresponding with her by letter," he announced. His chest puffed out like a peacock.

Robert burst out in laughter. "Jolene? Oh, dear God, this should be entertaining."

Grace thrust her thoughts into the situation. "I write her often, Robert, and she has not met another man. Why not let Alastair try? He is, after all, a fine gentleman."

"Because, love, they are nothing alike. I am afraid my feisty half sister will be quite bored with him, or she will attempt to change him in some fashion like she did me."

"Bored?" Alastair huffed. "I'm wounded to the core by my dearest friend's assertion." He placed his hand over his heart and sighed. "I will make a damn good husband for any woman who wants a tender, romantic man of integrity," he defended vehemently. "Would you rather she marries some sod like Geoffrey Chambers?"

Alastair rose to his feet and wandered over to the decanter. He needed another drink after that jolting remark. Robert followed and came to his side, placing his hand on his shoulder.

"No, of course not. I am sure you will make an excellent husband for any woman who will have you. If you think you can catch Jolene's eye, I wish you the best of luck." He paused. "Believe me, you will need it." Robert chuckled.

Rising from her seated position, Grace joined the two.

"Well, I for one think Alastair has every quality any woman would want in a husband." She leaned forward and gave Alastair a sisterly peck on his cheek. Turning to Robert, she sneered. "As for you, Robert Holland, that is a quality you will need to prove to me that you possess." She wiggled her index finger in his face. "I am not an empty-headed, silly girl, so be forewarned."

Alastair grinned watching Robert's confident smirk disappear.

"Well, I. . ."

"No need to answer," she replied, holding her hand up to halt Robert's objection. "I shall expect you tomorrow evening at seven o'clock sharp. Make sure you choose an expensive restaurant. I am very picky about what I eat and expect the finest of cuisine."

Grace lifted her skirt and turned toward the door like a grand lady. "I will leave the two of you alone to speak about womanly pursuits."

After she departed, Alastair regarded Robert. "And you think I'll need luck in my pursuits? Good luck with my sister, Holland. Frankly, you don't have the slightest inkling of her personality." Alastair gave him a hearty pat on his back. Robert shot a concerned glance toward the door, dropping his shoulders.

-·❋·-

As soon as Grace exited the parlor and closed the door, she brought her hand to her mouth and giggled aloud. Perhaps Jolene encouraged Robert again to spend time with her. Whatever the reason, her heart felt as if it would burst.

She ran up the stairs to her bedchamber and sat down in the window seat. The book, still in her hand, held no interest whatsoever. It was another romantic tale for her to daydream about for hours on end. Usually reading stories about other lovers put her in the doldrums. With Robert finally giving her an ounce of attention, she could not stop smiling. In fact, her cheeks hurt. She brought her palms to her face trying to soothe her muscles.

Her eyes surveyed the landscape while she mentally counted the years she spent cultivating a crush on Robert. The moment she first met him at sixteen, she lost her heart. Even though other young men had shown her interest in her coming out, she never found anyone else to excite her like Robert.

Alastair met him while at university where they forged a strong friendship. Along with Robert's cousin, they had become the three musketeers of sorts, playing with the affections of women. Though she never believed Alastair to be morally loose, he must have indulged in the spoils.

After she had turned eighteen, a remarkable event happened. Jolene von Lamberg, a komtesse from Austria, came to their home for a visit. They quickly forged a bond, whereby Grace confessed her feelings for Robert. Jolene encouraged her not to give up hope. To everyone's surprise, she later revealed she was Robert's lost half sister, who had been kidnapped as a baby. The news shocked social circles in London, and the poor Holland family once again became the object of gossip.

Nevertheless, nothing could keep her from Robert, no matter what whispering old women talked about behind closed doors. The fact he wanted to court her caused her heart to flutter. One day he'd inherit the title of duke from his father, and she would be a duchess. Finding a good husband was every young woman's pursuit, but being a duchess would certainly be a fairy tale come true.

A soft knock came at her door. "Enter," she replied.

Alastair peeked inside her room. "Can I come in and have a word with you?"

"Yes, of course." Grace rose to her feet. "No doubt you want to speak to me of Robert's intentions." She approached and grabbed her brother's arm. "Oh, Alastair, tell me he is earnest and will not trifle with my affections. You know how I feel about him."

"I've always been aware of your womanly emotions when it comes to Robert. All I can say is that I sternly warned him if he breaks your heart, he would answer to me. I will not be lenient with him." Alastair pounded his fist into the palm of his hand. "I swear I will break that nose of his into a million pieces."

"I promise you that I will not allow him to take liberties with me. You can trust me to keep my virtue," Grace said, lifting her chin in the air.

"Father and I have already spoken of the matter, and we both agree you are a sensible woman who can take care of yourself. Should he be less than a gentleman in your presence, wallop him up the side of his head."

Grace smiled. "He may find me more than he can handle, you know."

"And I've warned him. Be yourself, dearest. If he cannot love you for who you are, then he is not worthy of you. There will be another."

"Oh, Alastair," Grace sighed. "You are such an ideal and kind man. I do hope Jolene will accept your interest."

"Speaking of Jolene, do you have the address so I may correspond with her?"

"Well, did you come to give me your blessing about Robert, or is your visit merely for Jolene's post address?"

"What do you think?"

"I think I should make you wait for it. Besides, you advised me not to seem too eager," she said teasingly.

"Grace Whitefield, it is not nice to make your brother suffer," he moaned.

She walked over to her writing desk and sat down, jotting the address on a piece of paper. "Here you go."

Alastair snatched it from her fingers and smiled. "Do you think my desires are too lofty, Grace? I do so admire everything about her."

"No more lofty than my dreams of being a duchess." Grace rose from her seat and stood to face Alastair. "Now go write your letter."

He looked at the paper and smiled. "Thank you," he said, exiting her room.

"Good luck, dearest," Grace whispered. "Robert is quite right; you will need it."

CHAPTER 2

"Will that be all, my lord?"

"How do I look, Dudley?"

"Good enough for the ladies if that is your intent," Robert's valet said.

"There is only one special lady this evening." Dudley's eyebrows rose as he stifled a smirk. "Well, I'm not the man I was a year ago, am I? Besides, Father keeps badgering me to settle down and get married."

"If I may be so bold to ask, are you ready to settle down?"

Robert vacillated about his answer. Was he? Even though both his parents encouraged him to find a wife, he could not decide. Up until that moment, he had not actually taken the time to consider what he wanted. Since Jolene's departure to Austria with Philippe, his life veered into a new course of responsibility. At this point, getting married presented itself as the next logical course of action.

"Ready? I'm not sure if I am, frankly." Robert scowled. He twisted his neck and rolled his shoulders, trying to relax his stiff muscles from pent-up anxiety. "That is all, Dudley. You may go."

"Very well. As you requested, the chauffeur is waiting to drive you and the young lady to your destination this evening."

"Thank you."

Robert took one last glance in the mirror examining his attire. The roguish young man he once portrayed had vanished, and the reflection of a more mature individual met his eyes. In the past year he had come to grips with his responsibilities, accepting his future title and preparing for its demands.

Nevertheless, the fact of the matter remained that the family fortune dwindled, like those of many other aristocrats. To contribute to the estate expenses, Robert decided to pursue his interest in law. At the same time, his father turned his love of horses into a new business pursuit of breeding thoroughbreds for racing. Hopefully the duke's endeavors would provide a new avenue of income for the future.

As far as his mother's pursuits, she regularly wrote to Jolene. They were drawing closer to one another, which gladdened Robert. Being no less a miracle that she had been returned and the family healed, Robert felt only good days lay ahead for everyone. Unfortunately, he had not the time to write Jolene as often as he wished, but she seemed to understand his situation. Truth be told, he missed her presence at the estate. Perhaps a nudge from his mother and father to extend an invitation might prove worthwhile.

Ready for the evening, Robert descended the stairs. Before leaving, he entered the parlor to give his parting words to his parents, who were talking quietly.

"Are you off for the evening?" His mother smiled at him. "You look very handsome."

"You always say that, Mother," Robert replied. She constantly gloated over him at every opportunity.

"Your mother tells me that Grace Whitefield will be your companion this evening for dinner," his father commented. "An unusual choice, but I have no objection."

"She is an excellent choice and a beautiful young lady," his mother countered.

"Yes, I will admit that a year ago I may have felt different about her. However, Jolene has been prodding me to get to know her better. I am taking her advice so she will stop badgering me about the subject." Robert smirked.

"Ah, yes, Jolene. She has been a good influence on you," his father concurred.

"Well, then, I'm off and shall not be dining with you this evening. Good night," Robert said, walking toward the door.

"Enjoy yourself," his mother called after him.

As he headed outdoors, the butler confirmed all was ready.

"The car is waiting for you, my lord." Robert nodded and exited the residence happy to see the automobile polished and shining.

"Your destination, sir?" The driver opened the door, and Robert climbed inside.

"To Lord and Lady Whitefield's residence, and then into London. I will be dining at the Ritz this evening. Reservations are at seven thirty, so I do not wish to be late."

"Very well," he acknowledged.

Robert sat back, feeling fidgety over the impending evening. Polite and mature dialogue with women had not always been his forte, and he worried whether he could keep Grace's interest. Being such a superficial cad for so many years had robbed him of genuine and intelligent conversation with well-educated females. With a bit of luck, he could maintain a witty banter on a variety of subjects with Grace.

Of course, he often conversed with Jolene, but she was family. Courting a proper lady for the solitary purpose of marriage was a different matter altogether. If he did marry Grace, their union would be one of convenience if nothing else. Frankly, he could not comprehend falling in love. The thought of losing his heart over a woman stripped him of control, which in itself terrified the daylights out of him.

"God, I hope I know what I'm doing," he groaned, shifting in his seat.

He watched the landscape pass by his window, inching closer to the Whitefield's country estate. The season had ended in London and just as well. He preferred the country to the foul air hanging over the city. Though he rented a small flat near the law firm, he tried not to frequent the lodgings. One day the Holland estate would belong to him, and the responsibility for its management would fall upon his shoulders.

Robert pushed the distressing thoughts aside as he neared

Grace's residence. In a few more minutes, he would be in the presence of Alastair's sister. He needed to be a gentleman.

"Better be on my best behavior," he murmured under his breath. He imagined Alastair's fist aimed at his face and shuddered at the thought of its thrust straight toward his nose. If he did not treat Grace with respect, he could end up suffering a painful consequence.

— · ❈ · —

"Lady Grace," the butler announced. "Lord Holland is waiting for you in the foyer."

"Tell him I will be there momentarily." Grace pulled on her gloves while her lady's maid draped a light wrap over her shoulders. The evening would be cool, and she did not wish to burst out in embarrassing goose pimples.

"Have a pleasurable evening, my lady."

"Oh, I will Ethel. I have been dreaming about this night for years. To be honest, I feel quite confident the evening will go exceptionally well."

Grace descended the stairs and glanced at the front door. By the sneer on his face, Alastair appeared to be threatening Robert again.

"Leave the poor soul alone, Alastair," she said, approaching him. When Grace glanced at Robert, he stood stiff, blowing short breaths as if he were trying to gain control of his nerves. His anxious demeanor strengthened her resolve to take advantage of the situation. Even though her heart had fallen helplessly in love with him, she possessed a confidence Robert could not shake.

"Don't worry, Alastair, now go. Leave us alone," she said. Grace shooed him away like a fly.

"All right. I'll let you two depart." He flashed Robert another cautionary expression.

Grace wrapped her arm around Robert and tugged him to her side. "Pay no attention to him, Robert. You, of all people, know how he likes to tease."

"Yes, I'm quite aware," he replied. He sneered at Alastair's departing body.

As they climbed into the car, Grace sat a respectable distance from Robert. "So, where are we dining this evening?"

"Will the Ritz be to your liking?"

"The Ritz? I'm impressed, Lord Holland," she smiled, giving him a quick wink. "I've heard they roast a tasty Welsh lamb, which I should like to try."

"Then lamb it is, but I will probably peruse their culinary offerings a bit further before settling for lamb."

Robert looked out the window at the passing scenery, twirling a ring around in circles on his finger. After he had let out a sigh, he spoke.

"The weather has been agreeable, don't you agree?"

Grace rolled her eyes. *Their first time together, and he speaks of the weather.*

"I suppose," she replied, sounding a bit terse.

"Alastair tells me your parents are in Italy. Will they be gone very long?"

"A few months, I believe. Mother loves the Tuscany landscape. Father enjoys the food. Have you ever been to Italy?" Grace hoped he would find the courage to look her in the eye.

"Who me?" Robert answered, darting a gaze in her direction. "No, not yet."

"Do you think Alastair's attempt to win Jolene's interest will be successful?" Grace had become bored with topics of weather and travel and wanted something a little more substantial to discuss. Robert chuckled and shook his head.

"I don't know. He will have an uphill battle, I am afraid. I don't think she will consider him a suitable match."

"Well, I disagree," she replied. "He is exceedingly suitable."

"Oh, I didn't mean he's not appropriate, Grace. I agree he is one of the best. It is their personalities. As you know, she is very feisty and outspoken, and Alastair is rather quiet and introspective."

"You do have a point there, but they say opposites attract."

"So they say," Robert replied halfheartedly.

The car reached its destination, and Grace scanned the hotel with interest. It opened in 1906, but she never had the opportunity to dine or even come for afternoon tea. Notoriously expensive and catering to the rich of society, Grace felt pampered when they were escorted into the exquisite dining room with marble columns, ceiling frescoes, chandeliers, and floor-to-ceiling windows. The host led them to their table, and Robert commented.

"It is a rather impressive room," he said.

"Indeed," Grace whispered.

After being seated and handed the menu, Robert took no time in scanning his choices. "I see Welsh lamb."

"Yes, please order that for me," Grace replied, setting down the menu.

A waiter approached. "My name is Monsieur Dufour, and I will be your waiter this evening. May I take your order?"

"The lady would like your Welsh lamb, and I will order the pheasant. Please bring us a bottle of Pinot Noir." He glanced over at Grace. "Forgive me if I'm too presumptuous on the wine choice. Do you wish something else?"

"No, that's fine. I trust your selection."

After the server had departed, Robert fidgeted with his silverware and napkin. Grace watched his uneasiness with amusement. She always thought Robert to be a self-assured male. When they visited the London Tower with Jolene and Geoffrey, he appeared far more at ease. Of course, their time together did not constitute courting by any means. Perhaps he did not feel threatened then but apparently did now.

"Are you all right, Robert? You appear to be restless this evening."

Robert opened his mouth to respond when the waiter arrived with the chilled wine and two glasses. He poured one for each of them and then retreated.

"I am slightly out of sorts," he admitted in a low voice. Robert lifted his glass to Grace. "Let us toast to a relaxing evening of getting to know one another."

"Yes, of course," she replied. They raised their glasses and sipped their wine.

Robert sighed and then finally maintained eye contact with Grace. "I'm finding it odd that even though I have known you for many years, this evening has intimidated me quite severely." He lowered his head as if embarrassed about his confession.

"Well, I am surprised," Grace admitted. "I won't bite, you know. Moreover, I am not known to make a scene in public. You are quite safe with me."

"It is foolish, I will admit it." Robert gazed at her silently for a few seconds. "You look lovely tonight—like a golden goddess in this atmosphere."

Grace chuckled. "A goddess? Well, I have never been called that before," she pondered. "Although I have wished for many years that you would worship me." A coy smirk curled her lips.

Robert shook his head and grinned. "Your sentiments have been known to me for some time. Moreover, you are also aware of my caddish ways in the years gone by."

"Oh, indeed I am, and so is much of society. Nevertheless, I gather you wish to take a different path for some odd reason."

After sipping is wine, Robert set the glass down. He slowly reached across the table and touched Grace's hand.

"I am sincere about courting you and have every intention of being a gentleman during our time together."

"All right," she said. Her smiled faded, replaced with a guarded frown. "I am confused, nevertheless, as to why the sudden change of heart."

Grace felt his thumb slowly brush across her skin. His tender touch felt heavenly. She yearned for it for so many years, and now there he was—across the table and slightly starry-eyed.

"My priorities changed, and I no longer play with the affections of women. As I told Alastair, you are an attractive, intelligent female with a pleasing personality. I'm drawn to your goodness, Grace, and wish to see if our relationship will blossom with time into something lasting for the two of us."

Robert let go of her hand and beheld her with puppy-dog eyes that begged for a response.

"Well, I am flattered by your admission," Grace said. "Though I will honestly admit I am slightly leery of your complete change of heart when it comes to women. As I stated before, you will need to prove to me that you are a good catch, Robert Holland, regardless of my childish crush."

"Fair enough," he replied. A relieved smile spread across his face.

A few minutes later the waiter arrived with their dinner. Grace settled into a pleasant evening with the man of her dreams. Robert relaxed and transformed into an intriguing and confident male. She had loved him from afar for many years, but now she was the object of his undivided attention. There were no anxious thoughts over her chances of ensnaring Robert's heart. She knew for sure that one day they would wed.

CHAPTER 3

Grace expertly ensnared Robert sooner than he expected. Each engagement they spent together, she weaved another thread into his heart and tied an unbreakable knot at the end. Proving herself to be a crafty and intelligent woman, her wiles had weakened his determination not to yield to romantic notions.

On the other hand, she possessed a talent for challenging him to be a better man, much as Jolene did. Grace almost sounded like his half sister, and he wondered if they were corresponding via letter on how to bewitch and control him at every turn.

Robert admitted after some weeks that he had developed a deep fondness for Grace. Nevertheless, to keep his courteous promise of behavior, he did not express physical adoration. Even his deliberate, respectful conduct shocked him. On a few occasions Grace would wear a low-cut gown that cruelly tempted his resolve. Unlike other women, she had been endowed with an ample bosom, which often attracted the wandering eyes of men. Embarrassing moments of arousal occurred when he pondered how it would feel to cup one of her plump breasts in the palm of his hand.

He often gave her a swift kiss on her pink lips but never pressured Grace beyond that trifling show of affection. Robert knew his weaknesses when it came to the female body and prided himself on his successful strategies of seduction. To use them on

Grace would be cruel, let alone dangerous, lest Alastair discover his behavior.

As his high regard for Grace deepened, he did toy with the thought of proposing but hesitated. It would be too soon to announce an engagement, because he decided on a long courtship to make sure he made the right choice.

Eventually Robert invited Grace to dine with his parents at their estate. He wanted to express to his family his serious intent and wondered how Grace would handle the pressure.

When the two of them arrived in the evening, they joined his parents in the parlor near the dining room. His father had a drink in hand, dressed in his formal white-tie dinner attire. His mother looked stunning in the changing style of the day, which looked like another new dress.

"Good evening," Robert announced. He led Grace into the parlor with her arm wrapped around his.

"Oh, look at the two of you," his mother remarked, cooing like a pigeon. "It is so good to see you again."

"Welcome." His father smiled and then gave Robert an approving nod.

"Thank you, Your Grace."

"Please, let us put aside formalities. You may address me less formally. I'm sure you don't call my son Lord Holland," his father chuckled.

"Heavens, no," Grace responded. "However, I do use his title when I wish to give him a piece of my mind."

"Indeed she does," Robert added.

The gong rang, and the booming voice of their butler announced dinner. Robert noted Grace's calm demeanor. Her even-tempered disposition contributed to her unwavering confidence. Nothing appeared to shake her in the tensest of social situations, which Robert deemed an admirable quality.

After the first course had been served, his mother engaged Grace in conversation.

"How are your parents? Well, I hope."

"Yes, very well, thank you. They have taken a holiday and will be in Italy for at least another month."

"Thank goodness you didn't say Paris or my wife would be

prodding me for another visit," his father remarked with a smirk.

"You are very amusing, dear."

"My parents are always bantering with one another, but it's all in love, I assure you." Robert explained his remark lest Grace think it inappropriate.

"Has anyone heard from Jolene lately?" his father asked. "Robert, are you keeping in touch by correspondence?"

"Time hinders me from writing more often, but Grace frequently corresponds." Robert felt a pang of guilt for not making a greater effort.

"She is quite well from what I gather in her letters. You can be assured that she often writes about how much she misses Robert," Grace replied. She hesitated when she caught the eye of the duchess hoping for more. "And both of you, of course."

"My daughter has expressed it as well in her letters to me."

"Well, Mother, then why don't we extend an invitation?" Robert glanced at his father. "The estate has an entire wing that is not being used. Indeed, Jolene and Philippe will welcome the accommodations rather than a hotel."

"Philippe?" His father raised one brow and frowned at Robert. "Here, living under our roof?"

"Certainly, darling," his mother coaxed. "We can, at least, extend the invitation. Philippe may choose not to come if that's what you are worried about." She looked disappointed over his remark.

"I suppose it would bring no harm if we invite Philippe too," his father said. "I doubt that he will be inclined to accept anyway unless I am away on holiday."

Robert glanced over at Grace, who gave him a questioning look. He had not taken the time to tell her all the sordid details of his family's history. She had only been privy to the gossip of his mother being his father's mistress but suspected Grace knew nothing about the matter of the brothel. It was a well-kept secret.

"Will you invite them?" His mother reached over and touched his father's arm. One look at her pleading eyes, and his father could never refuse her requests.

"Yes, I will send a telegram in a few days and extend the invitation. Will that make everyone happy?"

"Indeed," his mother grinned. "Robert, I'm sure you will be excited to see Jolene too."

"I am, in fact," he said. "There are some matters I wish to speak to her about in private."

"What matters?" Grace cocked her head and looked at him curiously.

"Personal matters," he said. He was not about to speak of it at the dinner table, though he wondered if his parents surmised he considered proposing.

Grace enjoyed the dinner with Robert's parents. It was pleasant to converse with them casually, and she felt welcomed and accepted. Robert's comment regarding Jolene and the matters he wished to discuss tormented her thoughts the entire way home. Even though Robert held her hand, he seemed unusually quiet. Had he been thinking of proposing?

She concluded that dining with his parents had been the next natural sequence to take in their courtship. Certainly it had to be Robert's way of showing that he felt serious about her or so she thought. However, with her parents abroad on holiday, he had not given any indication to her father and mother.

With all the thoughts rumbling about in her head as she tried to guess what Robert was thinking, they began to breed doubts. In all the time that they had been together, Robert never said the word "love" nor had she for that matter. He knew how she felt about him, but perhaps she needed to articulate her affection. *No, that will not do*, she thought to herself. *I will place him in an uncomfortable position of reciprocating whether he means it or not. I shall wait until he declares his love first.*

If her growing doubts were not enough, Grace suspected that she was not attractive enough for his taste. He acted far too proper the entire courtship, and she became bored with his courteous behavior. Every woman wants to be swept off her feet with a passionate kiss now and then. She honestly expected a bit more aggressiveness when it came to romance.

Grace heaved a loud sigh, convinced that it was all Alastair's fault. He threatened poor Robert so many times she was sure he was afraid to suggest anything further. When she returned home, she would give Alastair a piece of her mind and demand that he encourage Robert to express his emotions.

"All you all right?" Robert turned and looked at her after hearing the frustrated puff of air leave her lungs.

His blue eyes looked darker than usual in the dim lighting of the backseat of the motorcar. In only a few minutes, the chauffeur would pull into their estate, and Robert would walk her to the door and bid good night. She would probably get another peck on the cheek.

"Why don't you ever kiss me passionately, Robert Holland? I truly adore you, but you are not meeting my standards in the area of romance. A lady expects more." There, she told him what was on her mind. If he did not scoop her up in his arms in the next few minutes and kiss her until she lost her breath, she might seriously consider breaking off the courtship.

"What?" Robert cocked his head and looked at her strangely.

"I'm quite aware that you have passionately kissed probably hundreds of silly women in your youth. Now here you sit, next to a woman who desires your affection, and you do absolutely nothing." Naturally, her lower lip extended in a pout.

"Well, Lady Whitefield, far be it from me to not give you what you want." Robert leaned forward, took her in his arms, and pulled her to his chest. His lips met hers in a heated kiss that drained every ounce of strength from her body. At last, the man she adored proved his physical desire. When he released her, he smiled at her like a roguish cad.

"Did my kiss take away your breath?" he teased. Robert traced his fingertip down the side of her jaw until it came to rest on her lips once again. "I would be happy to give you another, love, but the car is pulling up to your residence."

Grace swallowed the lump in her throat. As he walked her to the door, she stood in front of Robert and spoke her heart.

"I will never know if you desire me as a woman unless you show me. Please, no more childish cheek pecks or glancing, heartless kisses. If our relationship is to grow, I want the real Robert Holland and not a man afraid that my brother will break his nose."

Robert backed Grace up to the column by the door pressing his body next to her frame. Astonished at his action, she felt his arousal pushed against her pelvis.

"Should I continue to kiss you with such passion, my darling, I shall be a tortured man until we marry," Robert whispered in her ear.

"Marry? Well, you still need to prove you have met my standards before I think of marriage." She narrowed her eyes and gave a stern warning. "You have a bit of work to do before I consider you worthy of being my future husband."

The door opened, revealing Alastair. He scowled at their physical nearness. Robert hurriedly pulled away.

"Are you coming inside, or are you going to stand out there all night making a spectacle of yourself?"

Grace leaned toward Robert and gave him a peck on the cheek. "Goodnight, dear. I must not anger Alastair."

She stepped inside, and Alastair slammed the door in Robert's face.

Marriage, Grace thought. Robert suggested a future, but did he love her or was she merely a convenience?

"So how was dinner?" Alastair followed her up the stairs to her bedroom.

"I can't remember, frankly, because Robert gave me the most glorious kiss I've ever experienced as a woman."

"He what?"

After hearing that squawking question, she had no desire to argue the point. Grace entered her room and shut the door in Alastair's face.

"Now see here," he bellowed from the other side.

"Good night, brother!"

Grace walked over to her bed and flopped onto her back. After closing her eyes, she giggled aloud. "I love you, Robert Holland."

CHAPTER 4

Philippe Moreau stood in front of a tall mirror, eyeing his appearance. He tilted his head to the right and left, admiring his new suit. Eighteen months ago he would have donned a worn-out tweed coat that made him look like a pauper. Now he was living like a king.

"What do you think, Bernard?" Philippe glanced at his valet, who stood behind him adjusting the shoulders of his ensemble. As usual, his face remained stoic and noncommittal. He doubted that the man would ever warm up to his presence in the von Lamberg manor.

"It is a good fit, sir," his valet remarked. "The count used the same tailor in years past. He is the finest in Vienna."

Philippe kept his gaze on the mirror, viewing his valet's facial expression in the reflection. "I agree, and it is quite kind of my daughter to recommend his services."

Bernard made two quick swipes of his hand over his shoulder, brushing away a spot of lint. Philippe turned around and looked him straight in the eye.

"I know that I am no count, Bernard. There is not a drop of aristocrat blood in my veins, and I surmise that you find it offensive." Philippe attempted not to scowl at the man as he inwardly struggled with his bruised self-esteem.

"Not at all, sir. It is my duty to serve, not to question."

"Well, then, I thank you for your service," Philippe replied, nodding his head in deference. "And I sincerely appreciate that you are not questioning my presence in this house."

"Will that be all?" Bernard stood awkwardly rigid in front of him.

"Yes," he replied. His valet swiftly departed his quarters.

Philippe lowered his head suppressing the feeling of unworthiness that still gnawed at his stomach. He made poor decisions throughout the years, but returning with his daughter, Jolene, to Vienna had been one of the wisest. The dreary, lonely life of the past faded away as he settled into his new surroundings. Besides the luxury of his lifestyle, he had grown closer to his daughter.

After the burial of Jolene's aunt, they returned to Vienna. When he first walked into the grand home of Count von Lamberg, he felt awestruck by its opulence. After living in a small, dingy rental in a poor neighborhood of Paris, the transition from poverty to wealth had been an adjustment.

The servants of the household, including the butler and the count's former valet, did not welcome his arrival with open arms. Understandably, it must have been a shock to the staff when she announced him to be her real father. At first, Philippe encouraged her not to reveal their relationship to mitigate any rejection. Jolene would not hear of it. She held the opinion they would be expected to welcome him regardless of the oddity and circumstances.

Perhaps on the surface they appeared to do so, but Philippe deduced by their dark glances and whispered comments it was not the case. Most of the staff had served Count von Lamberg for decades. When Jolene offered Philippe her stepfather's quarters, he swiftly declined the offer lest the servants became offended. It was far too soon after his passing to usurp what rightfully belonged to the count. Surely it would appear disrespectful and presumptuous on his part.

Upon Philippe's arrival, the language barrier had proven to be a trial. Fortunately, the butler spoke a little French. The communication, though tedious at times, did occur. His valet knew little, and at Jolene's insistence, the butler tutored Bernard with what knowledge he possessed. After a year of training,

Bernard had become rather proficient.

On the other hand, the staff inquired of his daughter why he did not learn German. Living in Vienna and entering society necessitated his own schooling in the native language. Jolene took on the role of personal tutor, which he found both endearing and frustrating when he quickly learned her lack of patience. Nevertheless, Philippe used each day with her to make up for years lost, and his fatherly love deepened.

Upon their arrival in Vienna, Jolene met with Herr Wilhelm, her solicitor, regarding her discovery of being Philippe's birth daughter. Had the count another family member, they could have legitimately challenged her inheritance and title. However, he had no living relative, so the conveyance of wealth remained.

As far as acceptance into society, it had not been an easy transition. Jolene felt it her duty to attend social functions to keep alive the von Lamberg legacy. They attended a few gatherings together, but it soon became painfully apparent that Philippe would not be accepted into her inner circles. Jolene had begun to lose acquaintances as a result, but she remained firm and adamant that nothing would change.

Philippe exited his room and proceeded downstairs for breakfast when the butler approached.

"A telegram arrived for you, sir."

"For me? Are you sure that it is not for my daughter?" He could not think of anyone who would send him a cable message.

"No, sir, it is distinctly addressed to Philippe Moreau." The butler extended the envelope for his taking.

"Very well," he said, waiting for the servant to retreat before opening the correspondence.

"My wife and I would like to extend to you and Jolene an invitation to visit us at our country estate for an extended period of time. Confidentially, it is imperative that you come. There are serious matters that I wish to discuss with you in private."

Alarmed by the clandestine appeal received from the duke, Philippe scowled. He found it curious that the man should write such a cryptic message. Immediately he began to worry about Suzette. Had something happened? Was she ill? Had young Robert fallen into trouble? What else could it mean?

Frustrated over the unknown, Philippe shoved the note into his pocket and entered the dining room. Jolene sat at the breakfast table drinking tea and reading a letter.

"Good morning. You look rested," he said, attempting to greet her with an ounce of cheerfulness.

"I had a good night's sleep. I am not sure why I have been so fidgety of late," Jolene commented.

Philippe filled his plate with the breakfast selection on the sideboard. Once again, he passed by the German sausage that had been set out regularly for the past eighteen months. Apparently no one ever considered ham or bacon, or a better choice of pastries, for that matter. Frankly, he missed French cuisine.

After he had sat down next to Jolene, he began a conversation. "Another letter? Who from this time?"

Jolene shook her head and smiled. "Alastair Whitefield, I'm afraid. He has been writing to me every week for months now."

"He is one of Robert's friends, is he not?"

"Yes, and Grace's brother. She is the young lady that Robert is courting." Jolene laid the letter face down on the table. "I'll finish it later."

"The young man must have much to say to you if he writes each week. Do you reply?"

"Occasionally." Jolene smiled. "I am afraid he is attempting to win my heart, Father. Living so far away, I cannot take it seriously."

An opportune time arrived to inform her of the invitation. Philippe dabbed his lips with a napkin and then cleared his throat.

"I received a telegram this morning from the duke. The Holland family has invited us to visit and stay at their country manor for an extended holiday."

"May I see it?" Jolene's eyes lit with excitement.

"It is nothing more than the invitation. Nothing to see," he said. Philippe changed the subject. "It appears to me that if this young man is interested in you, this might provide a perfect opportunity for the two of you to spend time together."

"Oh, Father, how can I leave Vienna? I possess responsibilities."

"I have been thinking about that for the past few weeks,

actually." Philippe took a sip of tea to moisten his dry mouth before continuing. "Why don't we take an extended leave? I think it would do us both good. If you are concerned about vacating the residence for a few months, you can always rent it out."

"Rent it out? How long do you wish to be gone?"

"Long enough for you to find a husband perhaps," Philippe said. A sly smile spread across his face.

"A husband?" Jolene jerked her head in his direction. "Are you trying to marry me off?"

Philippe returned to his poached eggs and took a few bites, attempting to suppress his laughter.

"Well, is that what you are trying to do?" Jolene demanded, scrunching her brow. She picked up Alastair's letter and waved it at him. "He is a fine young man, but I have been with him once before. There was no spark."

"Oh, so that's your definition of male enchantment," Philippe said dryly. She definitely needed counsel in the area of courtship, he thought. "Is it a spark you seek foremost rather than a sound character in a man?"

"Well, like any other woman, I would enjoy an exciting, romantic, and attentive male. Were you not like that with Mother?"

Philippe practically choked at her question. After composing himself, he answered her inquiry.

"Your mother and I grew to love one another slowly by getting to know each other. I never behaved impetuously in her presence but sought to make a good impression upon her father. Early on I realized she deserved my respect and care, not my *spark* as you call it, bringing her to ruin."

"This is definitely disillusioning," Jolene replied, pouting over his admission. "I thought the French were more modern in their romanticism."

"Some perhaps, but your mother and I had not been brought up to be promiscuous," he curtly replied.

Philippe shifted in his chair irritated over Jolene's remark. It brought up wounding memories that Suzette had not kept herself but stooped to giving her virginity to a man he had despised. She was nothing more than a kept woman until he rescued her from his clutches. Jolene noticed his puckered brow as he ruminated over the past.

"Obviously I have upset you."

She reached across the table and touched his clenched fist. Philippe shook his head in exasperation.

"I worry about you. Love is more than a spark or an exciting physical attraction to a handsome man. If it does not have the foundation of respect, you place your future happiness in jeopardy."

Jolene withdrew her hand and lowered her eyes to the letter still clutched in her hand.

"Shall I respond and tell them when they may expect our arrival?" he asked.

"How long do you think we shall be gone?"

"Would six months be too long? If we outlive our welcome at the Holland estate, we can travel. I wouldn't mind seeing Scotland and Ireland."

Jolene silently pondered before answering. "Let them know we will come after we lease the residence. It will keep the staff occupied and employed during our time away."

Philippe eyed the letter, teasing his daughter. "So what does this Alastair have to say?" He tried to snatch it, but Jolene prevented him from doing so.

"I do not know because I have not finished it yet," she snapped, flashing an impish smile. "It would do you well to mind your business." Her usual arrogant chin lifted in his direction.

"Oh, I see," Philippe replied, playing her little game.

His attention returned to breakfast and the telegram hidden in his pocket. Hopefully they would be able to leave within a fortnight.

— ·❄· —

After breakfast, Jolene excused herself to walk in the garden. She was intent on finishing Alastair's letter, for it always contained news regarding Robert and Grace. Anxious to read if their relationship progressed, she discovered Alastair's heartfelt plea that he hoped to see her one day soon. Perhaps someone mentioned to him the invitation.

When the first letter arrived, she admittedly chuckled over the contents. He stated that Robert granted him permission to write, based on the fact he granted Robert permission to court Grace. The two sparred with one another, and the arrangement sounded quite plausible. By Alastair's admission, he threatened Robert bodily harm if he hurt Grace.

In her short time of knowing his sister, and from their exchange of correspondence, Jolene had no doubt that the young lady would give Robert a challenge. Jolene hoped that the two of them would eventually marry. Physically they made a handsome couple when standing next to each other. More importantly, Grace would be a good match for Robert's character. Jolene saw her as a stabilizing influence on his less than admirable tendencies she observed before.

Jolene tried to recall when she first arrived in London. The only recollection of Alastair had been their waltz at the ball while she yearned for that rake of a man, Geoffrey Chambers. Robert, Geoffrey, and Alastair were best of friends in pursuit of women. Nevertheless, Grace assured her that deep down Alastair was a man of character and not like the others. Remembering despicable Geoffrey made her shudder. *Dear Lord, I hope I do not see him while in England,* she thought.

Jolene sat on a garden bench and opened the letter. Alastair's penmanship was flawless. Not a blotch of ink or crooked line met her eyes. His thoughts filled the page with grandiose prose. Naturally, he attempted to impress her with his reputed good character. He never failed to compliment her on some aspect of either her appearance or personality. How could he ascertain so much about her with one family dinner and a waltz?

"Conjecture," she mumbled. "He must wish me to be this way."

She could not help but wonder if Robert and Grace were encouraging him on this path.

"Oh, perhaps I shouldn't be so judgmental." She shoved the letter back into the envelope and rose to her feet. Undoubtedly, he would vie for her affections as soon as she set foot on English soil. Possibly she would feel a spark this time instead of that dreadful feeling of having no interest. She hated to hurt his feelings, but Jolene did not want to settle for anyone.

Her father's words of caution to seek character floated through her mind. When remembering the insatiable passion her mother had felt for the duke and their illicit affair that it produced, she swore to never act so shamelessly. Even though she wanted the spark of romance and physical attraction, she convinced herself that she would never succumb to ruin.

CHAPTER 5

Jolene and Philippe exited the motorcar and were greeted by the family, as well as the staff lined up at attention to their left. No sooner had she set foot on the pebbled drive than Robert raised Jolene up in his arms. He swung her around like a rag doll and gave her a kiss on both cheeks.

"God, it is so good to see you!" His smile was contagious.

It took a moment for her to straighten her hat that he had displaced and regain her balance. "It's wonderful to see you too, Robert."

She glanced to her right and saw the duke shaking hands with her father and exchanging a few words. Suzette stood a few feet away smiling. Jolene felt no hesitation in approaching her mother and giving her a sincere hug.

"Mother, you look well. I'm so happy to be here."

"Oh, Jolene, how wonderful to see you again." Suzette leaned forward and gave her a kiss on the cheek, and she reciprocated.

"I see your father has taken good care of you, young lady," the duke said. Jolene hesitated to embrace him, and he appeared relieved.

"And you as well." She lifted her eyes upward toward the impressive manor house. The green countryside, warm sunshine, and chirping birds added to the welcoming atmosphere.

"Our staff will take care of your luggage," the duke

announced. "If you need anything at all, they are here to serve."

"Did you not bring your lady's maid?" her mother queried.

"No, we left the staff in Vienna because we leased the residence while on holiday."

"Well, we will quickly rectify her absence and provide a valet for Philippe."

They entered the house, and the footmen scurried about carrying their trunks upstairs. Her mother escorted everyone into the large sitting room, with floor-to-ceiling windows that flooded the interior with light.

"I had our cook prepare pastries for your arrival and a pot of tea." A footman standing by served the beverages, and everyone settled in for a few minutes of conversation.

"I had hoped that Grace would be here too. How are the two of you getting on, Robert?" Jolene looked at him fully aware that she put him on the spot. All eyes turned toward her half brother.

"Yes, how are you getting on, Robert? Your mother would like to know." Suzette playfully smirked.

"We are getting along very well, thank you," he answered. He opened his eyes wide and gave Jolene a warning glare that clearly conveyed his wish for her to dispense with further queries. "You needn't worry. Grace and Alastair will be joining us for dinner this evening."

"Dinner?" Philippe jumped into the conversation. "Is this the Alastair that has been writing to Jolene every week?"

"As a matter of fact, it is," Robert said. Jolene could sense that he was about to tease her in return. "So, how are the two of you getting on?"

Embarrassed, Jolene took a sip of tea. She straightened her posture and shamelessly answered. "The two of us are not getting on with anything. He merely writes to me, and I occasionally answer."

"Are you speaking of Alastair Whitefield?" Her mother took a keen interest in the conversation, leaning forward waiting to hear more.

Hesitating to respond, Jolene took another sip of tea. Robert detected her evasion answering the question.

"Yes, Alastair, I'm afraid, is quite taken with the komtesse."

"Really? Well, that is very interesting," her mother responded.

"Enough of potential suitors," the duke interrupted. "How have the two of you been?"

"I will let Father answer that question," Jolene responded, nodding her head at him.

"We are doing quite well. I will admit that my relocation to Vienna has been an adjustment. Jolene has been tutoring me in German, and the staff seems to be getting used to my presence in the household."

"If they are anything like our staff, they probably have their downstairs gossip sessions," the duke replied. "I trust they are treating you with respect."

"Yes, though my valet scowls at me occasionally," Philippe lightheartedly voiced. "I scowl in return."

Jolene suddenly yawned, unable to stifle the urge. She brought her hand to her mouth to hide her embarrassing action. Everyone glanced in her direction.

"Oh, dear, I'm sorry. It has been a long journey, and the lack of sleep is taking its toll."

"Well, then by all means let me show you and Philippe to your suites," Suzette offered, rising to her feet. "You have an entire wing to yourself."

"Let me accompany you," the duke added, "and I'll show Philippe his quarters."

Jolene thought it strange that the duke wished to escort Philippe. Her father did not seem to mind and looked as if he wanted to speak to him, anyway.

"Please, show me the way before I fall asleep in my teacup." Jolene took her mother's hand and squeezed it tight.

Robert came to Jolene's side and whispered in her ear. "Enjoy your beauty sleep. I am sure you will want to look your best for Alastair this evening."

"Really, Robert, must you tease me?" Jolene turned away toward the staircase and heard Robert call after her.

"What are brothers for?" he chortled.

--·✸·--

A soft knock came at the door, and Jolene stirred in bed. She glanced at the clock on the mantel and was shocked to see six o'clock. Jumping out of bed, she grabbed a robe.

"Yes, who is it?"

"Gladys, my lady. I have been asked to attend to your needs."

Jolene opened the door and saw a young woman she surmised to be in her thirties. She wore a black, uniform dress with a white lace collar. Her blondish, red hair was fastened in a bun on top of her head.

"Oh, please come in."

"Dinner will be served at seven thirty, but guests are arriving at seven o'clock. Shall I draw bathwater for you?"

"Yes, that would be wonderful. I cannot believe I slept for so many hours." She twirled around and looked at her trunks, which had already been unpacked. Her dresses hung in an open armoire, and the dresser drawers held her personal items.

"I hope you don't mind, your ladyship. While you were sleeping, I took the liberty of putting your things away."

"Well, you must have been quiet as a mouse. I didn't hear a thing," she said.

After the bathwater had been drawn, Jolene pampered herself with fragrant bath salts. It felt good to relax in the warm water after the long trip. She would have liked to lounge for an extended period, but she needed to get ready.

Gladys helped her dress in her undergarments and lace her corset. Jolene examined her choice of clothes for the evening. Not wishing to look irresistible to Alastair, she chose a modest, cream-colored evening gown with a square neckline. The top fabric of chiffon covered an underskirt of lightweight silk. The beaded bodice carried to the back of the dress, where the dressed opened to a V-shaped to her mid-backbone. The chiffon draped in angled layers down to the hem, which touched her matching silk pumps.

"What a beautiful dress." Gladys admired the fashion as she fastened the back closure.

"Yes, it is one of my favorites." Jolene pulled on her white gloves. The clock on the mantel chimed the seven o'clock hour.

"Oh, dear. I must go, or I'll be late." She pulled opened the door and rushed downstairs, trying to remember the location of the large sitting room.

"Lost are we?" Robert approached and gave her a kiss on the cheek. "My, my, you look absolutely stunning this evening."

"Now don't start teasing me," she warned.

"Here, take my arm, and I'll escort you. Our guests have arrived, and they are eager to see you again."

She had no idea what to expect in the evening ahead but felt uneasy at the thought of seeing Alastair. As they entered the room, Grace rushed toward her in enthusiasm.

"Jolene, it so good to see you again." She clutched both of her hands tightly.

"Your face is aglow, Grace. May I assume that is because of Robert's excellent treatment of you?" Jolene glanced playfully at him.

"I think we are good to each other," she replied. Grace stepped away to allow Alastair the opportunity to greet her. "Alastair has been anxious to see you again."

"It's a pleasure, Komtesse." He bowed his head in deference but maintained a solemn countenance.

"Hello, Alastair," Jolene replied. "I must say that your correspondence has kept me entertained these past few months. You are a very articulate man."

Jolene pulled her attention away from him not wishing to extend the greeting. Her gaze met her mother and father, who watched her interaction. Eventually everyone sat and chatted about the evening ahead. Determined not to encourage Alastair, she purposely did not often glance at him. Nevertheless, he did look rather fetching in an austere kind of way. She recognized a maturing stature in his face and mannerisms. Robert, as well, exuded a different persona. Grace displayed the same dreamy-eyed adoration she noted on her first visit.

"So what profession have you chosen?" her father asked Alastair. "Are you a solicitor like Robert?"

"No, sir. I do have a law degree, but I'm frankly more interested in politics."

"Politics?" Philippe's brow rose slightly. "Interesting

choice."

"He's a gentleman," Robert interjected. "Frankly, Alastair doesn't need to work. His family has been more fortunate than others in British aristocracy."

"Then he makes a good catch for some young lady," the duke added. He gave Jolene a quick glance as if to say she should pay attention.

Dinner was announced, and to Jolene's surprise, Alastair had been seated next to her. Philippe sat across the table while Grace and Robert sat elbow to elbow. The comments, seating arrangements, and prodding appeared like an orchestrated strategy.

"Did you have a pleasant trip?" Alastair leaned in to start a conversation while they sipped their soup.

"Yes, it was uneventful but tiring." Jolene felt obligated to cordially converse. "Thank you for writing so many letters. I enjoyed hearing the news about Robert and Grace's relationship blossoming."

"You are quite welcome. I'm sure you have gathered by now that I am very protective of Grace's heart."

"And so you should be," Jolene added. "It is an admirable quality to protect one's family."

"Jolene," Grace interrupted. "Robert and I will be attending a masquerade ball next week at Brentwood Hall. Both our families have received invitations. You should accompany Alastair. It would be such fun."

"Well, Suzette and I will not attend," the duke added. "Philippe, you may go if you wish to enjoy the revelry with the young people."

"I have no desire to dress like the Joker and attend a masquerade." He nodded at Alastair and Jolene. "The two of you should attend and have a night out."

"Oh, I agree," her mother chimed in. "Enjoy yourself."

Alastair shifted in his chair and fiddled with his silverware, clearly uncomfortable about the obvious matchmaking remarks.

"It seems that we have been paired as a couple to attend the ball. Do you mind?" he said, looking at her with a glint of hope.

Of course Jolene felt pressured. Everyone ceased eating and

looked at the two of them. How could she decline the invitation?

"No, of course not. I've never attended a masquerade ball." She smiled demurely and then glanced over at Grace. "You'll need to help me pick a costume."

"Well of course I will," she replied enthusiastically. "It will give us an opportunity to spend time together."

"Indeed." Attempting to appear excited about the preparations, Jolene smiled warmly in return. Spending time with Grace would be a comfortable occasion, but accompanying Alastair to the affair caused anxiety.

After dinner, the customary separation of males and females occurred. She retired to the parlor for tea with Grace and her mother, while the men lingered behind in the dining room for port and stinky cigars.

She would have preferred that the four of them not convene alone. No doubt they would be contriving how to bring her and Alastair together, or so she imagined. Jolene had already decided that Alastair was not what she was looking for in a man. Nevertheless, she knew it would be rude to dismiss the possibility to Grace and Robert, who undoubtedly hoped otherwise.

As she sipped her tea, a thought popped into her head. She gasped in horror over its arrival, sending liquid to that perfect place which obstructed her airflow. Quickly she set the cup down and coughed, attempting to suck in a breath of air.

"Good gracious," Suzette said, her face contorting in alarm.

Her mother reached over and instinctively gave her a few hard pats on the back, which frankly did not help much. After a few more gasps, Jolene felt relief.

"How silly of me," she said, feeling her face burn with shame. A few more coughs escaped her lungs.

"One must swallow first before inhaling air," her mother said lightheartedly.

"It's my fault. I had a horrible thought enter into my head."

"What thought?" Grace looked at her cockeyed.

"Geoffrey Chambers." Her mother's eyes grew wide in anger.

"That insufferable no-good boy," Suzette angrily sputtered.

"You don't think he will be at the masquerade, do you?"

Jolene shot a worried glance in Grace's direction.

"He might, but I wouldn't worry about it. With Robert and Alastair at your side, I doubt Geoffrey would be daft enough to even approach you after what he did in Paris."

"Stay far away from him," Suzette warned heatedly. "You would think that Lord Chambers would do something about his son, but all he does is encourage his despicable behavior. Marguerite enables him with support, making it even worse."

"Then no repercussions were forthcoming for his behavior in Paris, I take it?" Jolene shuddered at how close he had come to raping her.

"None that I am aware of," Grace added.

"There were minor repercussions," her mother added. "I believe he is now living alone in a rented flat, but Robert's sister insists that he be given a monthly allowance. Why I have no idea."

"Robert and Alastair have shunned him completely," Grace said. "They no longer speak to Geoffrey."

"I should think not," Suzette added. "It's a wonder that my husband didn't kill him that evening."

"Honestly, I would not be surprised if someone snaps one day and does murder the revolting man," Grace quipped.

"Well, I suppose I shouldn't be concerned. I trust Robert to watch over me." Jolene sighed, not wanting to cross paths with Geoffrey.

"You can relax because Alastair will be diligent to protect you." Grace reached over and patted Jolene's arm with a grin of encouragement.

"It is reassuring to know that they will both be at my side," she replied, not wishing to play into Grace's comment.

She picked up her teacup and took a small sip, making sure not to choke. Her mother and Grace both grinned at her like plotting Cheshire cats.

CHAPTER 6

Dressed like an Egyptian queen, Jolene felt out of place. Grace talked her into the outfit, but she thought it far too revealing. Her sentiments waned, however, when she arrived at a showcase of risqué-costumed women.

Alastair donned a seventeenth-century outfit looking like one of the three musketeers. With his thin mustache, he played the part well of a swashbuckling Frenchman. Grace and Robert went dressed as Romeo and Juliet. Robert appeared a bit miserable in his Elizabethan clothes, but Grace looked stunning.

When they entered the ballroom, an outlandish world of disguises filled the area. Masks differed from a mere covering over the eyes to fanciful feathered and bejeweled decorations worn by the ladies. Jolene chose a rather unadorned one in comparison.

In a matter of a few minutes, Alastair twirled her around the dance floor. The crowded room made the interior stifling. Catching her breath was difficult. Her skimpy costume at least gave her some relief compared to the voluminous dresses worn by other women.

"Thank you for accompanying me this evening."

Alastair glanced into her eyes with a familiar gaze of affection, which he had been offering her for the past week. His daily visits to the Holland manor consisted of afternoon tea and walks in the garden. She could not deny him the privilege of her company in case it appeared rude. Inwardly, Jolene did not welcome his frequent social calls, resisting his mild-mannered advances.

There was no denying that Alastair Whitefield possessed admirable qualities. Wealthy, always well dressed and groomed, he appeared as the perfect model of any woman's desire for an engaging beau. Alastair also exhibited protectiveness and loyalty to those he loved. Regardless of his good nature, Jolene found his keen attentiveness smothering. He rarely smiled, and on occasion, she would catch him brooding over what she surmised to be her lack of reciprocation. Though she felt encouraged by her family to spend more time with him, she really wished that she had the heart to express her sentiments.

"You are most welcome," she replied. She looked into his hazel eyes and feigned a warm smile. "It is hot in this ballroom, don't you think?"

"Indeed, it is." After the music had ended, Alastair walked Jolene over to a chair. "Would you like to rest while I fetch you refreshment?" If only she had a fan, she could push some air across her sweaty brow.

"Oh, yes, please do," she pleaded. Alastair quickly acquiesced to her request and left her shortly to fetch a cold drink. Jolene glanced around, searching for Robert and Grace. She spotted them across ballroom floor chatting with another couple.

"Well, well," a familiar voice spoke, coming up from behind. "Look who is back in England. If it isn't the infamous Komtesse von Lamberg."

Jolene jolted. She quickly rose to her feet and spun around. The raking gaze of Geoffrey Chambers peered at her from behind his black mask. Dressed like a Roman legionnaire, she wanted to stab him as Brutus had done to Caesar. Her fears of their paths crossing had come to pass. The despicable degenerate who tried to rape her stood only a few feet away.

"Leave me alone," she snarled.

"Really, Jolene. You have not changed a bit. Your arrogant air from the Continent oozes from your tantalizing body dressed in that outfit, oh queen of the Nile." Geoffrey bowed at the waist and then drew slightly closer. She could feel his hot breath on her face as he leaned in and spoke. "I would happily be your Anthony, my dear, if you were my Cleopatra."

"You unscrupulous beast," she growled from her throat. "I am so glad your uncle threw your carcass out into the street before you had your unwelcomed way with me."

Geoffrey reached out and grabbed her upper arm. His long fingers wrapped around her delicate bare flesh squeezing it tight. "You know you wanted it, you little whore." He eyed her up and down. "You even look like one dressed in that outfit with your breasts plumped up like two juicy melons."

Outraged by his remark, she tried to pull away, but he gripped her harder. "Let go of me!" While snarling at him and attempting to free herself from his painful grasp, her attention turned to an authoritative voice.

"Sir, the young lady has requested that you release her arm. If you do not do so in the next second, I'll be forced to rip yours from its socket."

His command boomed in Geoffrey's direction. Jolene lifted her eyes to the stranger, pleading for help. Geoffrey scowled, obviously intimidated by the ultimatum received from a dominant male. He dropped his hand and stepped back from her body.

"We were merely having a conversation," he snapped. "It's frankly none of your damn business."

"I make it my business when a man gruffly handles a woman. Now I suggest you leave before I'm forced to make a scene."

Geoffrey looked at Jolene in contempt. "Our conversation is not over. Another time, perhaps, we will have the opportunity to conclude it without interruption." After eyeing the man with scorn, he stormed off and disappeared into the crowd.

Jolene trembled and brought her hand to her chest trying to calm her rapidly beating heart.

"Are you all right?" The stranger's kind eyes emitted empathy, and his voice returned to a gentle tone.

"Yes, thank you!" She heaved a relieved sigh. "I don't know what I would have done had you not come along to rescue me from that…"

Her words trailed off not wishing to make an offensive comment in front of him. Having composed herself, she finally took notice that he looked like Robin Hood. The outfit accentuated his virile physique, which she found most appealing.

"My pleasure. I am always happy to assist a damsel in distress. Robin Hood and all that," he said, flashing a pearly smile. He paused and studied Jolene with interest. "I hope you don't think me rude, but might I inquire your name?"

Without hesitation, she gladly replied. "Komtesse Jolene von Lamberg."

"Ah, that explains the charming accent," he said. "Viscount Derrington at your service." He removed his hat and bowed at the waist. "I do hope this distressing incident will not spoil the remainder of your evening."

Jolene had forgotten about Alastair, who she spotted approaching with a drink in his hand. "No, I don't think so."

"Might I be so bold as to ask if I may have the honor of spinning you on the dance floor?"

Alastair arrived preventing her from responding. She desperately wanted to accept his invitation.

"Here is your beverage," he said. Alastair gave the unrecognized gentleman an inquisitive look.

Jolene took the chilled glass of champagne and took a sip to wet her dry lips. "Thank you. May I present Viscount Derrington?"

"A pleasure, sir," Derrington responded to the introduction.

"And this is Mr. Whitefield, who has been kind enough to escort me this evening." The brooding face that Jolene had seen before returned. "Perhaps I should explain, Alastair. While you were away, Viscount Derrington came to my rescue."

"Rescue, did he? From what?"

"Geoffrey Chambers, I'm afraid."

Immediately Alastair stiffened in his stance. His eyes darted about the ballroom looking for him.

"He roughly manhandled the young lady by her arm, and I felt compelled to intervene," the viscount declared.

"Well then, I thank you for protecting her from that scoundrel." Alastair stepped closer to Jolene as if to mark his territory.

"A young lady shouldn't be left alone in a crowd this size," Derrington said. It sounded as if Robin Hood had scolded one of his merry men for abandoning a female.

"She was parched and warm, so I asked her to sit and rest while I fetched a cold drink. I saw no harm in doing so," he defensively declared.

Jolene cringed over his aggressive, heated reply.

"Please wait here a moment, if you will," she instructed Viscount Derrington.

Jolene pulled Alastair a few feet away. "He invited me to dance, Alastair. I would like to accept if you do not mind. I really do owe him one dance for saving me from Geoffrey." She reached out and touched his forearm tenderly. "I hope you understand."

He dropped his shoulders and lowered his gaze to the glass in her hand.

"Yes, of course, Jolene. If you feel obligated, then by all means dance with him." Disappointment filled his eyes.

Perhaps Jolene should have apologized, but as she stood in front of Alastair, she felt drawn toward the handsome viscount who awaited her answer. His undeniable male magnetism robbed her of clarity. Pushing aside any thought of the hurt her actions might inflict upon her escort, she swiftly gulped her drink and handed Alastair the empty glass. He grasped it as she spun around to face the viscount, who flashed a concerned glance.

"I hope that I am not causing you any distress," he apologized. "It is not my intent to intrude into your escort's affairs."

"No, no. I spoke of my wish to accept your invitation to dance to thank you." Jolene inhaled a breath to calm her jittery nerves. "Would it be convenient to do so now?"

His dark brown eyes sparkled from behind the green mask. "I would be delighted." He held out his hand, which she eagerly grasped. Instantly, she found herself in his strong embrace, spinning her around the room.

-·✻·-

Robert and Grace enjoyed the evening chatting with acquaintances and occasionally dancing a waltz. After stopping for refreshment, they wandered over to Alastair, finding him unaccompanied. Robert saw the foul look upon his friend's face and knew something had to be amiss.

"You look as if you have bitten into a sour pickle," he said. "Why are you standing here alone? Where is Jolene?"

"Over there dancing with another gent," he answered morosely. Alastair nodded his head in the direction of the dance floor.

Grace's eyes darted around the ballroom. "Over there, Robert, to your left. Who is that man?"

Alastair turned his back to the waltzing crowd not wishing to see the spectacle. "He says his name is Viscount Derrington," he spewed.

"I've never heard of him," Robert replied.

"Nor have I," Alastair answered.

"Why is she with him?"

"I left her to rest a moment while I went to get her a glass of refreshment. While away, Geoffrey Chambers had a word with her and apparently gruffly grabbed her by the arm. Robin Hood came to the rescue."

"Oh, my goodness!" Grace gasped, bringing her hand to her mouth.

"Where is that bloody ass?" Robert's nostrils flared. His eyes darted about the ballroom. "So help me, I'll kill him if he touches her again."

"He disappeared into the crowd, I'm assuming, and I have not seen him." Alastair slowly turned around looking for Jolene. "I suppose there is no harm in her dancing with the stranger to thank him for intervening."

Robert finally caught sight of the pair. His sister's face radiated. The man definitely caught her eye, which confirmed his earlier suspicions that his sister would not be receptive to Alastair's pursuit.

"Well, it's just one dance," Grace commented. "It's not as if she's abandoned you for the entire evening." Her attempt to cheer her brother landed on deaf ears.

"I'm concerned that Geoffrey may be still lurking around somewhere." Robert continued to scan the crowd looking for his cousin. Of course, with everyone hiding behind masks and costumes, it proved impossible to pick him out of the gathering.

The waltz ended, and Robert turned his attention to Jolene, who walked arm in arm with her rescuer.

"Viscount Derrington, may I introduce you to my half brother, Robert Holland. The beautiful lady at his side is Lady Whitefield." Alastair stood silently as a mouse, sporting a suspicious look at Jolene's dance partner.

"A pleasure to meet you," Viscount Derrington responded. "And Lady Whitefield, may I assume that you are related to Alastair?"

"Yes, I am. He is my brother."

Robert glanced over at Grace to catch a silly smile on her face indicating her own keen interest in the handsome male. Surprisingly, a twinge of jealousy twisted in his heart at her reaction.

"I understand that you intervened on the komtesse's behalf," Robert said. "Thank you for doing so. I am ashamed to admit that he is my cousin, who possesses a rather distasteful personality."

"It was providence that I happened to be nearby to witness the incident. I found it most disturbing, but any gentleman would have intervened." Derrington glanced over at Jolene, and Robert caught the interest in his eyes.

"May I inquire of your family's origins? I'm not familiar with the Derrington name." Robert purposely pulled his attention back toward him.

"From the north, in York."

"York? You are a long way from home. What brings you to London?" Robert continued the investigation.

"Brother, you sound as if you are examining him in a court of law. Must you intrude into his personal life?" Jolene's surprise scolding caught Robert off guard.

"That is quite all right, Komtesse. To answer your question, I am here on family business." Viscount Derrington's curtness conveyed a slight irritation at the interrogation. "Now, if you will excuse me," he announced. "I will take my leave. It's been a pleasure to meet all of you." Before he departed, he turned to Jolene. "Enjoy the remainder of your evening." After those words, he left.

"You didn't have to scare him off," Jolene complained.

"I was merely making conversation," Robert replied in a cross tone.

"Oh, Romeo, I doth need another dance," Grace jested, pulling him away from the tense scene.

"Fine." Irritated over what transpired, he took Grace's hand and dragged her onto the dance floor. Frankly, he did not feel like waltzing, because his eyes were busy scanning the area for Geoffrey.

"You were a bit intrusive in your questioning," Grace said.

"You think?" Robert smirked.

"I found his presence irksome," she admitted.

He questioned her sincerity. "By the twinkle in your eye, you appeared to be enamored by the handsome Robin Hood." Robert pulled her tighter against his body, making his claim.

"Enamored?" Her cheeks flushed.

"You heard me."

"Oh, Romeo, you know I only have eyes for you," she teased, batting her lashes.

The glow on her face confirmed it to be true. Nevertheless, the incident had produced his first pang of jealousy where Grace had been concerned. The Romeo and Juliet costumes had definitely gone to his head.

CHAPTER 7

It did not take long for Alastair to pull Jolene back to the dance floor, claiming her by his side. Even though the orchestra played her favorite Johann Strauss waltz, her mind only thought of the charming viscount. With each twirl, her eyes glanced about the perimeter of the ballroom, hoping to catch another glimpse of the intriguing man.

Her attention drew back to Alastair by his firm grasp on her waist and crushing clutch of her hand. Jolene beheld his eyes, startled to see not the familiar despondency but rather resentment. Keenly aware that she had injured his ego over accepting the dance, Jolene attempted to allay his wounded emotions.

"It appears that Geoffrey has left," Jolene began. "As I glance around the ballroom, I do not see him."

"Is he dressed like a villain?" Alastair turned his dark gaze upon Jolene.

"A Roman legionnaire."

"I'm surprised he didn't dress like Julius Caesar. Then I could assassinate him with a knife in his back and no one would have cared." Alastair spit his sentiments, glancing about the room looking for Geoffrey too.

After he had made his comment, his clutch around her waist and hand increased to an uncomfortable level. Jolene winced.

"Your tight hold has grown painful," she whined. "Do you

mind?"

"Oh, I am sorry."

When the waltz ended so did his pressing grasp. Irritated at his cross emotions, Jolene stepped away.

"You are a very protective friend," Jolene said. "But you shouldn't say such dreadful things."

"Say what?" Alastair asked, looking at her oddly.

"Murdering Geoffrey," she quipped. Of course she fantasized about stabbing him as well but did not literally want to shed blood. If anyone had a reason, it was her. "I agree he is a disgusting man, but no one deserves to be murdered." Rather than offering an apology for his behavior, Alistair's eyes narrowed in response.

"Why do you scold me?" he countered. "Robert holds the same sentiments. We both are concerned about your welfare after his shameful attempt to ruin your reputation."

Mild-mannered Alastair had changed before her eyes. Astonished at his brusque attitude, Jolene no longer wished to converse with him or be at his side. It was obvious that he had lost his good sense on her behalf, and she wanted nothing more of it.

"Excuse me," she brusquely replied, pushing past him. "But I need some fresh air."

Jolene made her way through the crowded room, searching for a way out. She saw two double doors that opened to a veranda. After multiple apologies, bumping into guests and shoving her way through the crowd, she made her way outdoors. Finally free of the stuffy room, she closed her eyes and inhaled a deep breath. Her irritation eventually calmed, and she glanced at her surroundings.

The veranda bordered an expansive and beautiful garden of green that had been lit with torches marking paths into its interior of mature trees, hedges, and flower beds. A few couples escaped the affair to stroll about the grounds arm in arm. The peaceful picture lured her forward, and Jolene stepped upon the soft green grass. She wandered down a pebble path and lifted her head to see the heavens above lit with stars and a nearly full moon.

A couple to the left of the pathway paused and exchanged a

romantic kiss. The sight of the two lovebirds stirred a yearning in her soul. Jolene longed to experience the overwhelming emotion of love. She halted her step and watched silently as they enjoyed each other's embrace and warm lips. A wistful grin lifted the corner of her mouth.

"Obviously, neither of them mind showing their affection in public," a soft voice spoke, coming from behind her.

The unmistakable tone of a new encounter inflated her grin to a broad smile. She slowly turned around to see the viscount only a few feet away. The lights from the torched path sparkled in his eyes, and Jolene felt the magnetism pull her heart helplessly from her chest toward him. Once again, his handsome and commanding persona exuded an irresistible aura.

"Viscount," she calmly greeted.

"Komtesse," he replied, removing his hat, revealing his thick, black wavy hair. A gentleman's bow bent him at the waist as he continued his salutation. "It is a pleasure to see you again." He glanced about. "I don't see your escort." A slight frown of worry crinkled his brow. "Why are you walking unescorted in this beautiful garden amongst dark shadows?"

"We had a bit of a disagreement," Jolene admitted without guilt, lowering her eyes.

"Not over our dance, I hope," he replied, taking a step closer.

"No, nothing of that nature. We are not courting but merely friends," Jolene swiftly clarified.

No doubt Alastair felt they were more than acquaintances, but Jolene certainly was not ready to close the door of opportunity elsewhere. As she lost herself in the viscount's sparkling gaze, her heart flung wide open.

"Nonetheless, you should not be alone. After all, that unruly gentleman who grabbed you earlier could be lurking about seeking an opportunity to accost you again." He cast a worried glance to the right and left as if expecting Geoffrey to jump out from behind a bush at any moment.

Jolene had not thought of running into Geoffrey again when she spirited herself outdoors. The man was correct to caution her for not thinking sensibly of the dangers that could be afoot in a dark garden. As she gazed at his chiseled features and admired his muscular physique under the tights of the Robin Hood costume, she blamed the viscount for her negligence.

"You are quite right. I should not be wandering about alone in the dark," she said sheepishly.

"May I offer you my arm to make sure that you are under my protection?"

He extended it in her direction with a hopeful glint in his eyes. Jolene smiled at his gesture.

"You are most kind," she said, wrapping herself around his sleeve assured he did not pose any danger.

"Good, then I shall not worry about you any longer," he said, pulling her firmly to his side. "Why don't we take a leisurely stroll?"

As they took their first steps, Jolene noticed that the couple who had been kissing continued in their embrace. Only now her beau had her pushed up against a tree, and his body pressed flush against her frame. One hand pulled at her skirt along the woman's thigh as if he intended to lift it higher. Jolene found it impossible not to stare at the heated scene unfolding, which the viscount noticed too.

"Does it bother you that they show no qualms about showing their affections toward one another in public?"

"Bother me?" she said, thinking about his question. She paused as the young woman's uplifted skirt revealed her upper thigh. A second later she jerked her head away in embarrassment. "Not necessarily," she answered. Jolene's heart pounded in her chest at the thought of what the young man intended to do. "I would expect such behavior from Parisians rather than the English," she chuckled.

"Well, everyone expects such behavior from the French," the viscount snorted in laughter.

Jolene snickered at his comment since he was unaware that the blood that flowed through her veins was French.

"Do you find it offensive?" she countered instead. Jolene glanced at him in time to see a mischievous smirk curl his lips. She did not wait for his response. "By the expression on your face, I think not. It's a silly question to ask any man, frankly." He halted in his step.

"I find no offense whatsoever in two people who are in love showing their affections, regardless of their nationality."

The viscount's sincere voice gave Jolene no doubt of his opinion.

"What of your area in the world?" he asked. "You have not told me where your endearing accent originates."

Jolene thought of her convoluted past. She had been born of Parisian parents and raised by an Austrian count. She hesitated to explain the oddity of her origins. By all rights he was still a stranger, so she remained on the side of caution.

"I was raised in Vienna," she said. "From what little I've seen of couples in Austria, they do not show their affections so readily in public."

"Do you follow the same rule?"

"I don't understand." Mesmerized by his presence, she did not grasp the gist of the question.

"Kissing in public," he clarified.

"Kissing?" A blush burst upon Jolene's cheeks, and she pulled her eyes away from him in awkwardness. The horrid memory of Geoffrey Chambers's stolen kiss at the Tower of London flashed through her mind. It sickened her remembering how he tried to violate her in Paris.

"Your actions are quite perplexing," he said, interrupting her thoughts. Without warning, he took his finger and lifted her chin gently upward. His eyes penetrated her nervous jitters, and Jolene's mouth gaped open.

"Surely you have been kissed before," he said, raising an inquiring brow.

Jolene lost herself in the romantic setting. It did not take long for her eyes to rest upon his lips, pondering what it would be like to kiss him. Without further hesitation, she admitted her predicament. "Well, I..." She could not confess her folly about Geoffrey at the Tower of London. He had just rescued her from his clutches.

"Then I take it you have never been kissed," he concluded. "Would you like me to rectify that situation?"

The draw of his voice melted Jolene at his feet. His hand lifted her chin a bit higher as he lowered his head and fixated his gaze upon her parted lips. Jolene nodded, accepting his invitation, unable to speak a word. She closed her eyes as he approached. When their mouths came together, it was a gentle, sweet arrival of bliss. The nerve endings in her lips tingled like sparks, and for a brief second, she felt lightheaded. It caused her to lose her footing, and he swiftly caught her in an embrace to steady her stance then withdrew.

"Oh, dear! It seems that I have literally swept you off your feet," he jested with a coy grin. After he had sensed that she regained composure, he released her and took a step backward.

Jolene giggled and brought her hand to her mouth. A horrible urge to beg for another kiss tempted her desires, so she stifled the bold entreaty. The nearby couple lost their senses when a moan of pleasure escaped the young lady's throat.

"We really should move away from here," she said, cringing over the pleasurable groans.

"Perhaps we should," he agreed, offering her his arm. "It could incite me to attempt another kiss." His arm gave her a little tug close to his side.

They walked for a few more minutes, and to her horror, she spotted Alastair standing on the veranda watching the two of them. His discovery of her with another man had no doubt crushed his tender heart. An uncomfortable prick of regret at her insensitive behavior arrived. She halted in her step.

"I really should be returning inside," she said with downturned eyes. "My escort and half brother will be wondering at my whereabouts." Jolene longingly viewed him, hoping that he would not allow her to walk out of his life completely.

"I cannot kiss and leave you like this," he pleaded. "May I see you again?" He reached forward, took her hand, and held it tenderly.

The warmth of his flesh flowed up her arm and lodged in her heart. There could be no doubt that she wanted to know more about Viscount Derrington.

"I am staying at the Holland estate in Surrey. Do you know of it?"

He shook his head no. "I'm sorry, but I do not." After pausing shortly, he offered another suggestion. "Perhaps we could meet somewhere in London. I am staying at the Savoy Hotel. You can send word to me there, and the concierge will make sure I get the message."

"Yes, that would work," she eagerly agreed.

He smiled warmly at her. "We can eat lunch or dinner if you'd like and take another walk in a nearby park," his passionate voice offered.

His hand tightened on hers, and she responded likewise. "Yes, that would be most agreeable," Jolene replied. "I will send word tomorrow, but I must go now."

"It pains me that I cannot give you a departing kiss," he said, beholding her with adoration.

"Maybe next time," she teased.

"Then I shall settle for something else," he sighed.

Jolene watched him as he lifted her hand to meet his lips. The sight of his tenderness made her smile, but it quickly faded thinking of Alastair waiting for her return. Jolene took one last gaze into his amber eyes brightened by a nearby torch.

"Forgive me, but I must take my leave."

She sprinted from his side and headed for the veranda door not turning around to glance one more time at a man who so quickly captured her heart. She did not see Alastair in the doorway. When she stepped into the stuffy and boisterous ballroom, she glanced at the crowd. To her utter surprise, she discovered him waltzing with another woman. Rather than appearing disgruntled, it seemed he found a replacement to soothe his wounded ego. Jolene felt ashamed that she had treated him so poorly.

— ·❈· —

Alastair walked around the ballroom seeking Jolene to apologize to but could not find her. When he saw the open door to the veranda, he quickly made his way to the exit and stepped outside. His eyes darted about the grounds and stopped in time to witness Jolene kissing the man she danced with earlier.

The scene appeared so appalling that he felt as if she plunged a dagger into his heart. He watched the blatant display of affection in public. Rather than worrying if the man would take further liberties, Alastair's wounded heart turned enraged. Jolene's insensitive and brash behavior crossed the line of decency in his eyes. The affection he held for her faded under the moonlight sky.

"Have you ever seen so many stars?"

A woman's voice caught his attention, and he turned his head to see a young lady by his side. She was dressed like a Parisian can-can girl in a bright red dress, layered with ruffles. Black silk stockings covered her legs, decorated with a white garter above her right knee. A scarlet ribbon weaved through her blonde locks, and a red mask covered her flushed cheeks. To accentuate the charming picture, a feathered boa wrapped around her neck and draped down her chest. Rounded plump breasts bulged over her bodice that would entice even the most stellar of gentlemen.

"Yes, there are many stars," he replied, smiling slyly, "but none as bright as you, mademoiselle." He tipped his hat.

She giggled and flashed him a teasing grin. "Thank you, monsieur," she replied in a coquettish manner. "Are you enjoying your evening?"

"Up until now, no," he answered. "However, I have the distinct impression that things are about to change." He wanted to punish Jolene for crushing his spirit, and the opportunity stood before him dressed in flamboyant red. "Would you like to dance?"

"Dance?" She lifted her skirt, exposing her petticoat underneath and kicked her leg out front. "It is what I do best," she exclaimed, swishing her skirted ruffles back and forth.

Alastair grabbed her by the hand and led her inside. They entered the dance floor, and he pulled her close to his body. He found an empty-headed tart to enjoy while Jolene was off carousing with a complete stranger. *Two can play this game*, he thought.

"What is your name?" His eyes shifted toward her cleavage, enjoying the view.

"Catherine," she replied, fluttering her eyelashes at him.

It was apparent that Catherine wanted more than a waltz.

Alastair determined he would leave with another more willing companion. He was tired of Jolene spurning his attention at every turn. *Always the gentleman,* he grumbled inwardly. *It is about time I have a little fun of my own.*

"I'm Alastair," he said. He lowered his head and whispered in her ear. "It is a pleasure to meet your acquaintance, sweetheart."

He pulled away to see the expression in her eyes as she flashed a coy grin in return. It was definitely more than a waltz they would enjoy tonight.

CHAPTER 8

In the morning, Jolene reluctantly made her way downstairs for breakfast. As she approached the dining hall, she halted in the doorway, glancing around the room. Purposely arriving late, she hoped to avoid everyone.

Robert, the duke, her mother, and father were chatting amicably with one another. Her mother saw her in the doorway and smiled.

"Jolene, you are finally here. I told Robert you must have slept for a while to recuperate from the masquerade last evening."

She glanced at her half brother, who did not bother to raise his head in greeting. A lump formed in her throat, dreading what lay ahead. After going to the sideboard and taking small portions, her mother begged for her company.

"Sit by me, Jolene. I am surrounded by men who want to talk about nothing but politics this morning." Suzette patted a nearby empty chair.

Jolene sat down and glanced at her father. He appeared relaxed and peaceful. To her amazement, he settled into the Holland estate well. Even more surprising was that he sat there casually chatting with the duke as if they were old friends—a miracle indeed.

Robert, on the other hand, refused to make eye contact. Before leaving the ball, Alastair informed his friend that he would be departing with another woman. The reason, of course, had to do with Jolene's earlier despicable behavior with the viscount. As a result, the ride back to the Holland estate had been dreadfully awkward. Grace sat quietly not speaking a word, and Robert pulled his mouth aside as if he were attempting to hold his tongue. No verbal exchange occurred the entire way home. Jolene knew that Robert would not keep silent for long.

"Tell me about your evening. Did you enjoy yourself?" her mother asked.

Robert lifted his head and shot Jolene a frustrated glare.

"Yes, it was an enjoyable time, though the ballroom was a bit stuffy from overcrowding."

"The costumes must have been dazzling with all the colors," her mother remarked.

"They were. I have never seen such a variety." Jolene stuffed a forkful of eggs into her mouth. Frankly, she did not wish to talk about the affair lest Robert say something in front of the family to cause her embarrassment.

"Did you enjoy Alastair's company?"

Her mother glanced at her eagerly with a hopeful glint after her inquiry. Jolene wanted to crawl under the table. They knew from Alastair's frequent visits that he attempted to win her heart. How could she tell them what she had done the evening before?

"He is an exceptional dancer," Jolene finally spoke, keeping her eyes on her plate.

"Excellent. I am pleased to hear you had a good time," her mother replied.

"For the most part," Jolene said, thinking of her unpleasant encounter. To her surprise, Robert entered the conversation.

"Geoffrey attended," he announced.

The duke ceased talking to Philippe and swung his head in Robert's direction. "What the hell was *he* doing there?"

Robert glanced at Jolene and with a straight face answered the question. "Apparently while Alastair left Jolene for a moment to get refreshment, he approached and grabbed her roughly by the arm."

"He did what?" his mother yelled.

Jolene glanced at her father whose eyes turned a shade darker.

"Nothing happened," Jolene quickly clarified. "I'm perfectly fine."

Robert cocked his head and gawked at her in dismay. "Tell them the whole story," he snidely remarked.

Jolene lowered her head, moving her fork around in circles through her fluffy eggs. Everyone sat quietly waiting for an answer.

"A gentleman standing nearby intervened and told Geoffrey to unhand me," she said, blurting her words out in a rapid stream.

"And did he?" her father asked.

"Yes, he released me, rudely complained, and then retreated," she answered.

"Well, that was a gallant act," her mother added. "Do you know who the gentleman is who came to your rescue?"

Robert tried to suppress a snicker over her predicament. Jolene narrowed her eyes at him, knowing that he enjoyed her squirming in the chair.

"Viscount James Derrington from York," she replied nonchalantly as if the name meant nothing to her. However, when it came from her lips, all she could think of was his dreamy amber eyes and his soft lips that had encircled hers. She swore his taste on her flesh lingered.

"A family that I am unfamiliar with," the duke said thoughtfully.

Robert restarted the political conversation with his father and Philippe. *How kind of you to spare me*, she thought, glaring at him.

She finished her breakfast and rose from her seat intent on a quick retreat. Robert rose at the same time.

"It's a nice day," he said, nodding toward the window. "How about we take a morning walk, Jolene?"

By the squint of his eyes, she realized he did not intend to let her off the hook so easily. There would be no use trying to avoid the scolding any further. Frankly, she probably deserved it, so like a terrible tasting spoon of medicine, she swallowed the inevitable.

"Yes, that would be pleasant." She glanced at everyone at the table. "Please excuse us."

Robert met her at the dining room door and then wrapped his fingers around her wrist leading her to the terrace. He dragged her out into the sunshine to ruin the pleasant day.

"We need to talk," he gruffly announced. His eyes narrowed into slits of anger.

"I know, Robert." Jolene sighed. Her mind flitted back and forth thinking of excuses for her behavior, but she found nothing honorable to save her from the forthcoming reprimand.

"Excuse me for being so vulgar," he began. "But what in the hell were you thinking last night?" He stopped walking, grabbed her by the upper arms, and turned her around to face him.

"Well, it innocently started out as a single dance to thank the gentleman for saving me from Geoffrey. I thought I owed him that much," she blurted in a passionate defense.

"So how did it evolve from a dance to a kiss in the dark with a total stranger?" Robert glared.

"Oh, you know about that, do you?"

"Alastair told me."

"I don't know," Jolene blurted. "Alastair and I had an argument, and I needed some fresh air. You will admit the room was stifling hot."

"An argument about what?" His tone softened a bit.

"He said that he wanted to stab Geoffrey in the back with a knife, which I thought offensive." She paused and scrunched her nose. "It's not like I haven't thought of doing a few dastardly things to him myself, but murder wasn't one of them."

Robert shook his head and heaved a disgruntled sigh. "You really don't know Alastair, do you?"

"I do to some extent," she countered. "He's an attentive and loyal person."

"You are right about one point—he is the most loyal individual I have ever known. And you know what, Jolene?"

"What?" she sheepishly asked, scrunching her shoulders together bracing for the worst of it to come.

"Your inability to be loyal to him for one evening as your escort has severely injured his heart."

Jolene felt wretched. Her eyes moistened with tears knowing that Robert was accurate. Alastair had been loyal and kind to her, while she betrayed him in the worse way possible. If only he had not seen her indiscretion with the viscount. Even though she felt sorry for being caught, it did not mean she held any remorse over the magnificent kiss.

"I will apologize to him as soon as I can," she said, hoping that would please Robert.

"Apologize? You can try, but I doubt that he will ever trust you again," he voiced with conviction.

"Oh, Robert, I am so sorry, but as hard as Alastair tried to win my affections, my heart did not respond to his overtures. If I lie to him about my real feelings, wouldn't that be crueler? Surely that would be a greater betrayal. Don't you agree?" She babbled her questions one after another trying to save face.

A sour expression on his face betrayed his frustration. "Walk with me," Robert ordered, stepping forward.

Jolene followed reluctantly, and the two of them fell into a pondering silence before Robert turned the subject in another angle.

"Who is this viscount that so quickly turned your attention from Alastair?" Robert's tone continued to sound irritated.

Surprisingly, Jolene could not answer the question. She knew nothing about him except that he was from York. As she thought about it, the fact that she kissed him with such little knowledge made her actions appear even more scandalous. His charismatic presence clouded her good senses.

"I know nothing about him," she finally admitted. She turned her head away, glancing at a passing rosebush to avoid Robert's displeased countenance.

"You know nothing about him, but you saw fit to kiss him," Robert answered. "What were you thinking?"

"Oh, I don't know!" Jolene halted her step and faced Robert. "He discovered me alone outdoors. The viscount expressed his concern that he thought it unwise to be walking about in the dark after what happened with Geoffrey."

"Well, he did have a point there," Robert said. "I give him that much credit."

"He asked to escort me, and I agreed." It sounded perfectly logical to Jolene.

"So how did it escalate into a kiss?"

"It's a blur," Jolene said, trying to remember everything that happened. "We were talking about another couple nearby showing their affections in public. One word led to another, and he kissed me."

"And you let him," Robert replied with a scolding voice again.

"And if you must know, I liked it," she bellowed, shoving out her chin in defiance. There, she admitted the loathsome detail.

Jolene stepped away and walked toward a nearby rosebush to put distance between her and Robert. She ripped a petal off a full bloom and began tearing it into little bits while thinking back. The stroll with the viscount had been filled with intrigue and romance, and the atmosphere added to her weakness. Robin Hood in his tights, whose face she could not fully see because of a mask, oozed with charm. The stars, the music indoors, a couple nearby kissing and making love, it felt like she had been lured into a garden of temptation. A snake probably dangled from a branch in a nearby tree watching her indiscretions. Robert remained quiet digesting her admission.

"Well, it's over now," he concluded. "You should at least apologize to Alastair, and then everyone can move on."

Still staring at the bush, Jolene could not believe Robert's comment. He made no mention of her spending time with the viscount again and assumed the affair was over, but it was not. How could she walk away from the opportunity to see him again after his invitation? Their encounter had dropped a seed of hope in her heart that she'd finally met an interesting gentleman. She could feel it grow even as she spoke of it to Robert. There would be no way that she would pull it out and throw away the possibility of love.

Jolene turned around and observed Robert. It pained her, but she knew to avoid his further reprimand, she needed to tell a little white lie.

"Yes, we can move on," she replied. Jolene lowered her eyes in a dejected manner, playing the part.

"I apologize for being so gruff with you, Jolene." Robert stepped forward, gave her an unexpected hug, and then pulled away. "The manner in which you behaved shocked me, frankly. I thought I knew your character." He cocked his head to the right, expressing affection in his eyes.

"Well, perhaps we are still learning about one another. Eighteen years apart is a long time. We only spent a few months together before I returned to Austria." Jolene lowered her eyes. "I'm not without my faults."

"And neither am I," Robert admitted with a sly grin.

She wondered about his relationship with Grace but did not want to pry, feeling drained of emotion. All she wanted to do was return to her room, sit at her writing table, and pen a note to the viscount for delivery at the hotel. She was about to act upon her faults—her desire for an irresistible man.

CHAPTER 9

For the past half hour, Grace allowed Robert to kiss her lips until they swelled. Satisfying his insatiable hunger for intimacy had been a challenge, to say the least. Of course, she had no one to blame but herself ever since she dared him to express his desire.

As the minutes passed, he lowered his head and kissed the roundness of her breasts, spilling over her bodice. Grace tilted her head back, fighting the temptation to let him do the unspeakable. Robert's breathing increased, and he placed the palm of his hand on her right breast, squeezing it gently. Even though her parents were away on holiday, she worried that Alastair would enter the sitting room at any moment or the butler for that matter.

"Let me sleep next to you tonight," Robert suggested with a seductive voice.

"You know I cannot let you visit my bed. I won't be able to resist you, and I shall be ruined," she sulked.

"Ruined?" He grinned mischievously. "You will hardly be ruined, my dear. I will gently open your bloom, and you shall be transformed into a beautiful flower."

"Open my bloom, indeed," she scoffed. "I suppose that is one way of saying you wish to take my virginity."

Robert gave her breast another kneading with the palm of his hand. "Let me taste your nipple," he passionately pleaded, pulling the bodice of her dress down.

Grace's eyes widened at his suggestion. Before she could protest, Robert tugged the fabric until he exposed her completely. With the skill of a rogue, he cupped her breast in the palm of his hand and encircled his lips around her nipple.

It happened so fast that she could not protest. He sucked with the proficiency of a skilled Casanova, and his hot hand held her flesh, fingering her until she thought she would go crazy. Unexpectedly she heard the front foyer door open and shut.

"Robert! Stop!" she heaved. Grace pulled his hand away and in one quick movement shoved her breast back into place. "Do you want Alastair to give you a black eye?"

Robert shot up like a bullet and sat next to Grace on the divan. He tried to straighten his shirt and tie but could not do so in time. Grace was horrified to see her brother standing in the threshold glaring at the two of them.

"Holland, what are you up to with my sister?" Alastair bellowed.

Poor Alastair, thought Grace. The challenges of the past few days left a pitiful appearance upon his face. Dark circles were under his eyes, his hair was in disarray, and his words were slurred. She did not need to ask if he had been drinking because she could smell the liquor on him from six feet away.

Robert rose to his feet. "Being affectionate but respectful," he said as an expert liar.

Grace nearly choked at his answer but agreed to go along with the ploy to save herself too. "Kissing. All we were doing was kissing," she said, unable to stop her cheeks from flushing bright red.

"I find that hard to believe," he mumbled, narrowing his eyes. Alastair walked over to a nearby chair and plopped on the seat. He brought his hand to his head as if he had a headache.

"What are you doing to yourself?" Robert angrily demanded. "You look like shit."

"Don't bloody swear in front of my sister," he reprimanded in return.

Grace laughed. "You are both so amusing," she said, leaning back into a comfortable position on the divan. She glanced down at her bodice to make sure that everything was still in place. When she realized that her skin was red from Robert's kisses and roving fingers, she cringed. Hopefully Alastair would be too drunk to notice.

"You're out late tonight," Robert remarked. "Did you take that lady out you went home with the other evening after the ball?"

"No," he said. "I was at the casino for a few drinks and a game of roulette."

"You know Mother and Father hate it when you gamble," Grace interjected. "Did you lose much?" Alastair said nothing. He stared blankly at Grace as if a void sat between his two ears. Apparently, he could not remember if he won or lost. "You better snap out of this Alastair before our parents return," she warned.

"I fell in love with Jolene," he moped. "Why did she have to go off and kiss the viscount whoever he is?" He held his head in his hands and moaned.

Grace and Robert exchanged glances. Robert took the lead and tried another tactic.

"So who was the girl you picked up at the ball?" he inquired in a lively tone.

"She was a tart, all right. Frankly, I think she was a prostitute who found a willing customer."

Grace's mouth gaped open. "Alastair Whitefield, don't tell me you bought a prostitute for the evening?" Her brother raised his head and regarded her with shame.

"Well, I probably could have had a good romp with her, but you know me—always the gentleman." His voice cracked. "What good it does me."

"You should go to bed," Grace scolded. "You'll feel better in the morning."

"Fuck, Holland," Alastair blubbered. "You have parted many thighs, and you are a hell of a lot happier than I am!"

Robert jumped to his feet and placed his arm underneath Alastair's, raising him to a standing position. "All right, that's enough," he commanded. "You are going to bed."

Grace caught Robert's mortified glance. Clearly worried that she had been offended by her brother's remark, she gave it no thought. After all, she had been well aware of Robert Holland's reputation before she nurtured an incurable crush. Frankly, that was part of his intrigue and challenge, conquering the rogue. Convinced that she almost won the victory, she let the comment slide. One day he would be her husband.

The two headed for the staircase, and Grace followed. Robert nearly dragged her brother the entire way and then steadied his sway to his room. He flung the door open and led Alastair to his bed. A second later he landed face first on top of the mattress.

"You should call his valet to tend to him," Robert said. "Otherwise, he'll wake up in his clothes in the morning."

"I will after you leave," Grace answered. She led Robert from the room and then closed the door.

Robert grabbed her hand and starting tugging her down the hallway. "Which one is your room?"

"Wouldn't you like to know," she said, pulling him to a stop. "You better go home, Robert Holland, before you get us into trouble."

He smirked and then pulled her into his arms, giving her a sweet kiss. Afterward, he whispered in her ear.

"As you lay under the covers alone tonight, remember what you are missing," he teased.

Grace peered into his blue eyes, and a surge of affection welled in her heart. God, she loved him so much that her chest ached. Robert's eyes showed his affection in return, but he had not spoken the words she longed to hear. Of course, she had not found the courage to tell him either.

"You look like you want to say something," Robert said. He reached out with his fingers and pushed aside a stray curl that had fallen on her cheek. "Are you angry with me for my forwardness this evening?" His eyes dulled, and she wondered if he felt remorseful for exposing her breast.

"No," she answered. "I'm not mad. It is just… I just…" The words would not escape her mouth as her lips tightened with fear.

"What?"

His inquisitive stare melted her resolve, but she lowered her eyes. If she did not speak her mind, the possibility remained that she could end up a spinster forever. After inhaling a deep breath, her tongue loosened.

"When you were touching and kissing my… well, you know, my…"

"Breast," he interjected.

"Yes, that." After a slight ill-at-ease pause, she continued. "I wanted to tell you that I loved you." She cringed at her blundering confession. Terrified that he would balk at her words, she was surprised to see a slow, sweet smile brighten his face.

"I am glad," he said sweetly, "because my loss of control is entirely your fault, Grace Whitefield." He gathered her into his arms and then tenderly spoke. "It's probably about time that I admit my weakness." He embraced her tighter. "I love you too."

A release of joy flooded Grace's heart. She flung her arms around Robert's neck. "Oh, I'm so relieved," she said with tears glistening in her eyes. Their bodies pressed against each other aroused Robert, causing her to giggle at his reaction. Swiftly he pulled away realizing she detected his physical state.

"I better go, or I'm going to pick you up and walk into one of these rooms and have my way with you."

Grace gave him a tender glancing kiss and smiled. "Yes, you better, or I may let you have your way with me."

He grinned and then ran down the stairs as if he were escaping a fire. Ecstatic that he had professed his love in return, Grace returned to her room to fantasize about Robert lying next to her in bed.

$$- \cdot \maltese \cdot -$$

Grace arrived at the dining room the following morning to find Alastair drinking coffee. Although sober, dark circles under his eyes revealed his miserable state.

"Experiencing the repercussions of too much alcohol this morning?" She smirked.

"Lower your voice," he demanded. "My head is pounding."

"Serves you right." Grace sat down at the table. The footman poured her usual cup of morning tea while she took a piece of toast and covered it with marmalade.

"Did you behave yourself with Holland?" Alastair raised his eyes and gave her a weak brotherly glance of concern.

"Yes, I behaved." A smile burst across her face. She could not hold in her happiness a second longer. "He finally told me that he loved me."

"He what?"

"Said he loved me."

"Did you tell him first?"

"What does that have to do with it?" Grace retorted, annoyed. She knew that he was trying to infer that Robert said it because she spoke it first. "It doesn't matter who said it first. He meant every word."

Alastair squinted at her dumbfounded as if he did not believe it. "Are you two going to get married?"

"Well, I hope so, though he hasn't officially asked," Grace said with a tone of disappointment.

"Love," Alastair complained. "I'm never going to love another woman as long as I walk this earth." He held out his empty cup to the footman who quickly filled it with more coffee.

Grace glanced at him sympathetically. "Robert said that Jolene intends to apologize."

"Really?"

"Will you forgive her?"

"I don't know," he grumbled, lowering his head. "I'm surely not going to pursue her like a fool any longer. It's useless." He frowned at his black cup of coffee. "Besides, she's probably falling all over the viscount."

"Maybe not," Grace said. "Robert is under the impression that the matter is over and done with. It was merely a poor decision on her part."

Alastair threw his napkin down on his plate and rose to his feet. "My head hurts, my heart hurts, and I feel like…" He halted, refraining from cursing in front of Grace. "I'm going to lie down for a while."

"Don't give up, Alastair," Grace encouraged. "Perhaps she will come around. Do you want me to talk to her?"

"No!"

His bellowing answer startled Grace. "Fine, I'll leave things as they are," she said, shoving a piece of toast into her mouth.

As Alastair stormed out of the dining room, Grace pondered the situation. Honestly, as much as she loved her brother, she was not surprised either that he did not win Jolene's affections. If only she could find a nice girl for him, it would make things much better. For the next few minutes, Grace pondered all her female acquaintances, considering the possibility of becoming a matchmaker. Surely there had to be a young lady out there somewhere who would catch Alastair's eye.

"I think Robert needs to give him some lessons in womanizing," she mumbled under her breath. Grace glanced at the footman, standing at attention by the sideboard who tried not to snicker.

"Well, it appears as if I have my work cut out for me," she announced. Grace took another bite of toast and plotted her brother's rescue.

CHAPTER 10

Jolene glanced around the lobby of the hotel looking for James. After privately corresponding by courier, they had chosen a date and location to meet. He instructed her to look for a man in a gray suit rather than a Robin Hood costume, which she though humorous. In his hand he promised to be holding a dozen white roses.

It did not take very long to spot him standing a few feet to the left of the front desk. Jolene halted for a second, taking note of his features without a mask. The viscount's presence in the lobby was undoubtedly the most impressive of all the patrons and staff. His dark hair, amber eyes, and commanding facial features were striking. The expensive, tailored suit accented his physique and broad shoulders. His magnetism drew her forward without hesitation or anxiety. He caught sight of her approach and smiled warmly.

"Komtesse," he greeted. He reached for her hand, and she lifted it for his taking.

"Viscount," she replied. "It is good to see you again." He kissed her gloved hand.

"I am blessed to be able to gaze upon your entire face," he remarked. His approval over her appearance glistened in his eyes. "How beautiful you are. As much as I enjoyed the ball, you must promise me never to cover your features again."

"Thank you," she demurely responded.

Jolene, somewhat embarrassed over her thoughts about how attractive he appeared, lowered her eyes. As she did so, she noticed that her fragrance and his cologne blended into a pleasing mixture.

"Oh, these are for you," he announced, handing her the bouquet.

Jolene took them and sniffed the baby roses. "How kind," she said. "They are pretty." The brilliant blooms were fresh and delicate.

"I have reserved a table at the restaurant," he said, nodding toward the entrance. "May I offer you my arm in escort?"

Gallant and handsome, Jolene accepted it. She laid the bouquet on one arm and wrapped the other around him firmly for support.

"Viscount Derrington," he announced to the host. "I have a reservation for two at one o'clock."

After a quick look to confirm the entry in his log, the host took two menus and led them to a table tucked away in the corner of the room. Thankfully, he had the foresight to ask for privacy, giving them an opportunity to talk uninterrupted. She took a seat and laid the flowers on the side of the table.

The host handed their menus, and Jolene opened to the selections cautious not to gaze at her companion too often. Happy to be in his presence, she discovered his aura intimidated her somewhat. She had embarked into the unknown territory of male pursuit. Though she exuded her inexperience in such matters, there could be no doubt in her mind that the viscount possessed vast familiarity. Her thoughts were confirmed when she lifted her eyes and caught him gazing at her with recognizable male pleasure.

"Have you dined here before?" Jolene asked, trying to get his attention to the menu. "Is there anything that you would recommend?"

She noted that he finally focused on the menu, pondering the selections. His inability to concentrate corresponded with her simultaneous wandering thoughts.

"Give me a moment," he finally replied. "My attention has been held captive elsewhere." He smirked.

It was impossible not to smile at his comment. Jolene perused the menu but realized she lost her appetite. Nothing appealed to her with her stomach fluttering about like a thousand butterflies.

"I'm usually not this indecisive," Jolene said, folding up the menu and setting it down. "Unfortunately, I do not possess an appetite. Would you mind if I ordered tea and finger sandwiches?" She lowered her eyes in embarrassment over her jitters. If she ate anything more than a few bites, her stomach might turn sour from nerves.

"No, that's quite fine. Actually, I ate a bit too much for breakfast this morning. It would do me well to have a small portion as well," he replied. The waiter arrived at the table to take the order, and he took the liberty of ordering a variety of tasty sandwiches, fruit, and a few sweets.

After the server had departed, Jolene relaxed before turning her attention back to the viscount. To her surprise, he nervously moved the silverware on the tabletop as if he needed time to gather his thoughts as well.

"I do hope that I am not the cause of your loss of appetite," he said. He repositioned himself in his chair in search of a relaxing pose.

"Please, call me Jolene," she said. "And no, you are not the cause of my lack of appetite."

"Good. Glad to hear of it." He smiled warmly. "I must admit that I was delighted to receive your note agreeing to meet. After I had left the ball, I was genuinely concerned that I might never see you again."

Jolene did not know what to say, but as the waiter returned with their tea, it gave her the chance reflect. A part of her worried she might appear too eager for his company.

"Well, after your gallantry in saving me from an unsavory gentleman and my unwise and unescorted stroll in the garden, it occurred to me that I owed you quite a bit." She tried not to act like a coquettish woman, but something about him made her want to flirt. "I wanted to spend more time with you."

His eyes brightened while his lips pressed together with a contented grin. "It is hard for a man like me to admit such weakness, but when I met you, an undeniable adoration filled my heart."

The emotional confession caught Jolene off guard. Her smile faded over his rapid expression of sentiments. Though she saw no lustful intent in his eyes, Jolene felt wary of his sincerity. When he noticed her change in demeanor, his eyes filled with concern.

"Forgive me," he pleaded. "I did not mean to sound overly forward. Perhaps I should rephrase my statement that an undeniable curiosity filled my heart."

"No matter," she said. "I accepted your invitation to see you again out of my curiosity." Jolene took a sip of tea, hoping to pull away from his intense scrutiny. He did so as well, but not long afterward continued his inquisitiveness.

"Are you in London on holiday?"

"Yes, from Vienna with my father. We are visiting family."

"The Hollands?" He looked at her keenly. "I'm a bit jumbled," he said. "You are clearly Austrian by your accent, yet they are family?" His brow scrunched showing confusion.

"The duchess is my mother, Lord Holland is my half brother. My father is Philippe Moreau from Paris." She closed her eyes listening to her own voice and the convoluted explanation of her past. How could she ever explain the mixture of English, French, and Austrian to a stranger?

The viscount stared at her blankly as if his mind tried to process her answer. By the look in his eyes, he could not make any sense of it.

"Well, now, I am confused," he admitted. "You are an Austrian komtesse with a French father. Are you or were you married to a count?"

Jolene giggled. His deduction of her status was plausible. "I know that my answer must sound ludicrous to you. My past, however, is quite strange, I assure you." He leaned forward as if he wanted to reach out and touch her hand. Jolene nervously withdrew it.

"I implore you," he said. "Enlighten me before I go mad attempting to piece the puzzle together."

"All right," she said confidently. She might as well come

straight to the point. "I was kidnapped as a baby. My abductor married my stepfather, an Austrian count. She died when I was three, and the count raised me."

"Kidnapped?" His mouth dropped open. "How terribly dreadful."

"Yes, for those who lost me, of course, but my life with my stepfather, Count von Lamberg, was blessed beyond measure."

"I see," he replied thoughtfully. "He must love you very much."

Jolene lowered her eyes to her plate. "He passed away a few years ago."

"Is that why you are now with the Holland family?"

"It wasn't until over eighteen months ago that I discovered that Robert Holland was my half brother and the duchess, my mother. Finally, after years of being apart, I was also reunited with my real father."

A blank gaze returned to the viscount's eyes as he attempted to process the revelation. He shook his head and smiled. "Well, this is going to take some time to sort in my mind," he admitted with a grin. "Now I'm even more intrigued how you discovered your identity."

"And what of you?" Jolene changed the conversation. She did not wish to spend the entire engagement focusing on her odd past.

He laughed. "I'm afraid that my past is quite ordinary and dull compared to yours—no kidnappings or lost family members."

"What brings you to London?" Jolene was curious why he traveled from York and how he ended up at the ball. It was apparent that he had not escorted anyone to the affair, which she found even more curious since he was a handsome and virile man.

"As I mentioned before, family business," he said, pulling his eyes away from her gaze.

Obviously, he did not want to discuss the reason further. Jolene thought little of it, concluding it could be anything from finances to personal problems. Even though he had not mentioned it, a sudden fear that he might be secretly married arose.

"I see," she responded. "And tell me of York. Unfortunately, I have never traveled north of London."

He fiddled with his silverware momentarily and then lifted his eyes. "Well, you should definitely take the train and explore other regions of England. The countryside is quite beautiful."

"I imagine that it is," she said. Jolene fell into a pondering silence, wondering where to take the conversation next. It appeared that he wished to remain private regarding his affairs. Of course, she could not blame him. Everyone had the right to privacy. The English were not exactly known for discussing their secrets with strangers, even though they appeared to love to gossip about the secrets of others.

Finally their order arrived, and Jolene immediately took a small sandwich to nibble on. The break gave her a chance to gather her thoughts, but she noticed he looked distressed.

"Forgive me for being forthright in my requests," he started, furrowing his brow. "But I do not wish that this short lunch be our only interaction."

"Oh?" Jolene grinned, hopeful over his impending suggestion.

"I am to be here at least for another month before my responsibilities return me home. During that time, I would be most honored if we could spend more time together."

Jolene examined the sincere eagerness in his gaze. "I would enjoy that, Viscount," she replied.

"James," he interjected. "Please, call me James."

"All right… James."

The familiarity of his name coming from her lips felt sweet, which she decided to use when fondly thinking of him. Even though he was somewhat private and guarded, Jolene could not deny she wanted to know more about him. She felt drawn, and it was apparent to her by his words and behavior that he felt the same.

The opportunity for possible courtship and polite conversation with someone that she was actually attracted to seemed captivating. Of course, Alastair had kept her busy and occupied for weeks, but that was different. As gentlemanly kind as Grace's brother had been in every way, she found him uninteresting, and nothing could be done about it. She did not intend to waste any more time for a spark to ignite between them when it had definitely ignited elsewhere.

Romantic love remained a far-off notion, which she had only seen affect other women—like her mother's desire for the duke. Would this encounter take her down the same path? If it did, it could be a dangerous route that she feared would consume her without reason. Just thinking about enjoying another kiss and embrace from the viscount caused her to shiver in anticipation.

"You looked distracted," he said, pulling her from her musings.

"Oh, I'm sorry. I was thinking..." Jolene halted. She couldn't tell him her private musings.

"Good thoughts, I hope." James reached out and touched her hand. She made no effort to pull away.

"Yes, good thoughts."

He stroked his thumb tenderly across the flesh of her skin, causing a tingling sensation. Jolene struggled with swirling, intimate imaginations.

"*La Bohème* is playing at the Royal Opera House," he said in a low voice. "Would you like to attend?" He lifted his eyes and looked at her with anticipation.

"Oh, I would love to," she replied with a coy grin. "It is one of my favorites."

"I could get tickets for tomorrow night's performance if it is not too soon."

"Tomorrow?" In her enthusiastic acceptance of his offer, she had not thought how she would explain it to her family. Robert's scowling face flashed through her mind, along with a certain worried frown from her father. Would they allow her to go alone with a stranger?

"I sense something is amiss by your hesitation," he said as his smile faded.

"Well, not amiss," Jolene confessed. "I will need to tell my family of our appointment and fear that they may not approve."

"Will they require a chaperone?" He asserted his concern. "By all means, if you must bring someone with you, please do so. I have no objection."

Jolene sighed. "Well, perhaps my half brother and Grace will agree to accompany us. The Hollands do have a box at the opera house, which I'm sure we can use for the performance."

James's brow furrowed, and he lowered his head. Once again, he played with his silverware. This was the third time he had done so, which was obviously a habit due to some slight insecurity on his part.

"Of course," he began in a low voice. "I would prefer to spend the evening with you alone." He gulped and looked at her with worry. "What if he doesn't wish to attend or forbids you to come alone with me? I… I…" he trailed off in a faint mutter and shifted in his seat uncomfortably.

James's concern already churned around in her own head. She knew that everyone would be overly protective, which was the very reason she lied about her whereabouts at that moment. A feigned excuse of needing a driver to take her to London to shop and visit the Whitefields had been what she conveyed to the butler a few hours ago. She told him to inform her father of her whereabouts but fled without saying a word of goodbye to anyone. Thankfully, Robert had gone to the law firm.

"All I can do is ask," she replied sadly. "However, I am a grown woman and can make my own decisions. If I must break protocol to be with you for an evening at the opera, then I will do so." An air of indignant determination lifted her chin.

"I admire women with a mind of their own," he remarked.

After another half hour of idle chat, Jolene glanced at her watch, noticing the lateness of time. She instructed the driver to return at two thirty. However, she could not return empty-handed when she told everyone she had been shopping. It was time to go and spend a few pounds on frivolous items to take home and then stop at the Whitefields to take care of the apology she owed Alastair.

"I beg your pardon, but I must be going," she announced. Jolene laid her napkin down at the side of her plate and picked up the beautiful bouquet of roses.

"If you must, then I understand," he said. James signed the check to charge the luncheon to his room and then rose from his chair. He stepped behind Jolene's and pulled out hers as she rose to her feet. "Let me walk you through the door," he said, offering his arm.

As they stepped into the lobby, Jolene felt dreadful. She did not want to leave. Their short rendezvous has sped by like a dream. So many unanswered questions about his life lingered in her mind. Their conversation, for the most part, had been superficial and unsatisfying.

"I will send word first thing in the morning by courier to the hotel regarding the opera. Will that be sufficient?" She gazed into his sorrowful eyes.

"Yes, that will be all right. I hope that your family will be agreeable to our meeting again."

James reached for her hand, and Jolene lifted it for his taking. He looked at her adoringly and then kissed her fingertips.

"I thoroughly enjoyed our time together and eagerly hope that we may have many more days ahead to delight in each other's company."

"As do I," Jolene said with a yearning smile. "I will find a way." Jolene closed her eyes for a brief second, burying into her memory the sight of his face. People buzzed about the lobby as they stood by the doors unaware of their encounter. One way or another she would see him again, even if she had to lie to be in his presence. "Good day," she finally said.

Jolene stepped outdoors into the fresh air and headed up the street to shop. She dreaded each step that she took in the opposite direction of the hotel away from James Derrington. Love at first sight had always been a cliché that she never believed—until today.

CHAPTER 11

After spending a few pounds on unneeded items at Selfridge, Jolene instructed the driver to take her to the Whitefields and wait. She promised Robert that she would apologize to Alastair for her dreadful behavior. Nevertheless, little remorse stirred her conscience as she stood in the parlor of his residence waiting for him to appear. If she had not taken the course of action of dancing with the viscount, the possibility of an exciting relationship would have never presented itself.

Jolene heard footsteps approach. Apprehensive, she nervously spun around and witnessed Alastair halt at the threshold. His eyes beheld her dolefully for a few seconds, and then he approached.

"Komtesse," he blandly addressed her. "What brings you here today?"

Jolene took a self-justifying stance. He knew why she had come to see him. "May we have a moment to talk?"

"If you insist," he replied.

Alastair gestured toward a chair, and Jolene quickly sat. She expected him to choose a nearby seat, but instead he stood a few feet away. His morose countenance portrayed his ill-felt sentiments that he did not wish to be in her company. An uncomfortable pang of fault finally stirred her emotions. As she pondered how to overcome the awkwardness of the situation, he spoke.

"What is the matter you wish to speak about?"

Jolene hated that he glowered above her small frame, so she rose to her feet and looked at him eye to eye. When she did so, Alastair took a step back.

"I owe you... I owe you an apology for my behavior the other evening," she stuttered. His eyes shifted toward her, narrowing into a hostile glare.

"No doubt you are here because Robert sent you. Frankly, I don't think you have an ounce of remorse for your behavior in abandoning me at the masquerade."

Highly agitated, she had not realized he could betray such overt annoyance. The revelation startled her, reminding Jolene how little she really knew about his personality.

"Yes, he asked me to apologize," she readily admitted. "I fully intended to do so even before his prodding." She stood her ground defensively, ignoring his daunting demeanor.

Suddenly Alastair walked over to the window. He turned his back toward her and remained silent.

"I am sorry," she admitted, sounding sincerely contrite. "I didn't take your feelings into consideration." Her voice trembled. "My behavior was appalling."

As she remembered James's kiss, it was not that appalling, she thought to herself. On the contrary, it was sublime. The earlier sense of guilt vanished as she thought about his engaging character instead.

Alastair shoved both hands into his pockets and turned around. The hard lines in his face displayed his injured emotions. Jolene, however, saw something else in his eyes that made her feel absolutely dreadful—unrequited love.

"I accept your apology for your insensitive behavior," he said crossly, "but I shall never trust you again."

"I know," she admitted. "I deserve your sentiments."

He pulled his hands out of his pockets and took a few steps in her direction. He towered above her, and Jolene timidly lifted her head and looked into his eyes.

"Part of it is my fault," he admitted. "I fell in love with you and should have known better."

"Oh, Alastair," Jolene moaned. His admittance placed a

burden of regret upon her heart. She opened her mouth to speak, but he held up his hand as if to stop her from saying anything further.

"You need not reply to my confession. I shall bear it and get over you." Surprisingly, a smirking grin lifted the corner of his mouth. "It's not as if I'm the last man on earth to have been spurned by a woman he loves. There is a reason we Englishmen maintain a stiff upper lip."

At that awkward moment, Jolene admired his character. Robert and Grace were right in all aspects of his kind heart. Nevertheless, as she searched inwardly for an ounce of amorous affection, it had already been captured and claimed by another.

"You are a good man," she admitted with heartfelt emotion. "You will make an excellent husband to another young lady."

He looked into her eyes, studying her intently. "I will make a good husband," he agreed with confidence. "My intent is to be a loyal, tender, and an understanding spouse. The woman I marry will be showered with my love."

He sounded as if he wished to convince her of what awaited. Had she agreed, she feared he would drop to his knee and ask to marry her then and there. She could not give him feigned encouragement.

"Surely there is a young lady who will love you wholeheartedly and appreciate everything you do for her." She turned her head away from his heartbreaking reaction.

"But that woman is not you," he remarked with his voice cracking. He paused to regain his emotions and then threw an unexpected question. "Have you seen him again?" He arched one brow over his right eye as if he already knew the answer.

Should she lie? Should she tell him the truth and risk further harming his tender soul? As she paused, he shook his head and stepped away.

"You do not need to answer," he announced. "I can see it in your eyes."

"Alastair, I—"

"You are thinking with your heart and not logically," he grumbled angrily. "You know nothing about this man, and yet you are throwing yourself at him after one kiss in a dark garden."

His comment hurt, and her defenses rose. "I can take care of myself," she said, turning away and heading for the parlor door. "This conversation will only evolve into an argument, and I do not wish to spar with you further."

Alastair reached out and grabbed her hand as she passed by him. He pulled her to a halt and coolly looked into her eyes. "Be careful," he admonished her. "I don't wish to see you ruined."

Ruined? Jolene had not entertained the possibility of being ruined. Her meeting the viscount brought nothing but the peaceful anticipation of a bright future.

"I take offense to your remark," she quipped. "I don't intend to let him take advantage of me emotionally or physically."

"Regardless," he huffed, "I do not have a good feeling about his intentions." He squeezed her hand tightly. "He could be dangerous."

Jolene jerked away, fuming over his assertion. "How dare you make such accusations regarding a man you know nothing about?"

She spun around, saying nothing further and retreated from the parlor. After exiting the front entrance in a blind fury, she barked at the driver to take her back to the Holland estate. He opened the car door, and she climbed inside. As she sat down, Alastair stood on the threshold of the doorway, watching her departure with an audacious glare. Jolene refused to maintain eye contact and fiddled with her hat instead.

The car pulled down the avenue, and she settled back into the seat. If Alastair acted so vehemently against her interest in James, she worried what Robert would think. No doubt her mother and father would sternly warn her as well. If the duke had anything to say about it, she would pay no attention. After all, they were not blood related.

Jolene hardened her resolve, knowing that the stubbornness of her personality would see her through. Nothing and no one would dissuade her from pursuing more time with Viscount Derrington.

--·❈·--

Alastair stood helplessly by, watching as the car pulled away. For a few minutes he stared at the empty street while ruminating over Jolene's angry departure. When he realized that his fists were clenched at his sides, he relaxed his fingers and let them dangle. The most important woman in his life slipped away from his grasp. Jolene would never be his, and his chest felt as if a brick replaced his beating heart.

"What are you doing standing at an open door?"

He heard Grace's voice and spun around. Not wishing to appear foolish, he swiftly closed it and tried to smile. Weakly, the corner of his lips turned upward.

"Nothing of importance," he muttered. "I thought you were taking a nap." Alastair brushed past Grace, avoiding her eyes.

"I heard voices," she said, following him. "Loud voices. Yours and I thought Jolene's."

When Grace followed him down the hall like a puppy dog seeking a tasty treat, he decided to stop and tell her the truth.

"You are right. Jolene came for a short visit," he said. "Go back to bed and finish your nap." Shaking his head, he looked at her up and down. "If Robert would bring you home at a decent hour, you wouldn't be sleeping in the middle of the day." It felt right to scold her over that point in the hopes she would leave him be. Instantly his sister set her jaw in irritation.

"Don't take your broken heart out on me," she spat.

Alastair grimaced at her testy response and wondered where he could escape in order to clear his mind.

"I'll be in father's study," he announced. His heels clicked down the tile hallway heading for a sanctuary, but Grace continued to follow.

"Why did she come?" She reached out and grabbed his upper arm. "Stop and talk to me, Alastair!"

Her voice echoed down the hall as he reached the door. Without stopping to answer her question, he turned the doorknob and stepped inside. A decanter of brandy caught his eye on a side table. He headed straight for a glass and poured himself a hefty amount. It would be impossible to convince Grace to leave him alone, so he justified the need for a stiff drink.

"Honestly, I don't wish to talk." The glass reached his lips, and he took a gulp. Unfortunately, it would take a few more glasses to numb his painful emotions. "Bloody women," he spat. "Look at what she's done to me," he railed, turning toward Grace. "I cannot keep my hand from shaking."

"Oh, Alastair," Grace moaned. She stepped nearer and placed her calming hand on his forearm. "Why don't you sit down, and we can talk about it."

It did not take long for Alastair to find a seat and plop on the cushion, slouching in defeat. He brought the glass of brandy to his forehead and closed his eyes.

"She came to apologize for abandoning me at the masquerade."

"Did she sound sincere?" Grace asked, sitting down in a nearby chair.

"Sincere?" He glanced at his sister, questioning whether she had been sincere or not. "Her voice trembled as if her remorse was heartfelt, and I accepted her apology with reservation," Alastair admitted. "Then I made an utter fool of myself and ruined everything."

"What did you do?"

"I told Jolene that I had fallen in love with her," his crackling voice answered. He felt like he wanted to crawl into the hole from stupidity.

"Oh, dearest, you didn't," Grace said, leaning forward. "What did she say?"

"The usual buggered platitude. One day I would make an excellent husband to some other woman." Alastair inhaled a deep breath, holding back unpleasant emotions he did not wish to express in his sister's presence.

"Did you say something discourteous to Jolene in return? Why did your voices rise as if you were arguing?"

Alastair shot up from his chair and walked over to the decanter.

"You do know that getting drunk will not cure your problems," Grace scolded.

"Stop mothering me," he said, setting the empty glass down on the tray. "I'm not getting another."

"You still haven't answered my question," she reminded

him.

Alastair took a few steps but felt too anxious to relax in a chair. He paced and then halted to speak.

"I merely told her to be careful with the viscount."

Grace grimaced. "I'm assuming that did not sit well."

Alastair shook his head. "No, not one bit," he answered. "She is bullheaded, which makes me wonder why I love her at all."

"Why do you?" Grace pointedly inquired.

Shocked by her thoughtful question, he struggled to answer. How does any man explain love? He could not even explain it to himself. What he did know is that physically he lost all control of his faculties when she neared. An odd sensation swirled inside his stomach and a warmth filled his chest cavity. There were instances that he found himself mesmerized by her beauty and barely able to speak. His mouth would go dry as if it were stuffed with cotton. If those manifestations were not enough to bewitch him, the terrible yearning for her love in return never ceased. He wanted her as any man wanted a woman and felt no shame fantasizing what it would be like to make love to her for hours on end. Obviously he could not express such personal sentiments to his sister, so he turned the question upon her out of curiosity.

"Why do you love Robert?"

"Now, that's not fair, you scoundrel," she whined. "I'm not about to share with you what I feel about him and my intimate thoughts."

"Then I cannot express to you my sentiments about Jolene," he countered. Then the worry returned for her safety. "I fear that this man will break her heart."

"Well, hopefully she will have enough sense to be careful," Grace said. "I'm sure that Robert will watch her like a hawk and will not allow the viscount to harm her in any way."

Alastair's brow arched as he considered Grace's statements. "Perhaps, but there is an uneasiness in my gut."

Grace giggled. "Probably jealousy."

Alastair frowned and shook his head negatively. "No, it's more than that."

"Well, there is nothing you can do about it," she said.

"Maybe, but I have half the mind to hire a private detective to have him followed." Alastair walked over to his father's desk and sat down in the large leather chair contemplating the possibility.

"You wouldn't," Grace replied, leaning over the desk and looking him in the eye.

He would. If he could not have Jolene for himself, it didn't mean he no longer cared for her welfare.

"You mean to do it, don't you?" Grace badgered him. "I suggest you tell Robert your plan."

"Say nothing to Robert. At least not until I'm sure."

"Very well, Alastair." Grace pulled away from the desk and adjusted her posture. "I care about you, dearest. Do be careful with your soul. You know that I only wish the best for you."

"I know." He snorted, finally feeling an ounce of levity. "So tell that lover of yours to bring you home at a decent hour."

"Very amusing," Grace replied. "I'm going back to my nap."

CHAPTER 12

Philippe retreated to the library early afternoon. The window afforded an unobstructed view of the lane leading to the estate. It had been hours since he discovered Jolene had departed the residence. According to the butler, she asked for the chauffeur. Without a proper companion at her side, Philippe pondered her whereabouts and safety. He already lost her once, and the thought of losing her again preyed upon him relentlessly.

To make matters worse, Suzette displayed deep disappointment that Jolene did not ask her to come along. The insensitive action on the part of his daughter disappointed him, and he fully intended to confront her once she returned.

As the days progressed since their arrival at the Holland estate, Philippe discovered the animosity he held toward the duke dissipated. There had been some enjoyable conversations with Robert and his father while sharing brandy and cigars after dinner. On the other hand, Philippe found the duke's behavior baffling at various times. He caught him gazing at Suzette, displaying a worried frown. Frankly, he did not know what to think but sensed that something unspoken was amiss in the household. He purposely did not bring up the inference in the telegram as a matter of good manners. When the duke was ready, he was sure the conversation would ensue at the appropriate time.

Young Robert, for the most part, returned to the estate on the weekends. He maintained a flat in London, which he frequented during the week due to the demands of his job. Frankly, he held a bit of fatherly pride in the young man, even though he was not his birth father. Robert had become a responsible and industrious young solicitor, who appeared to be on the brink of marrying a fine young lady.

As he pondered Jolene's life and search for a future husband, his attention was drawn to an approaching motorcar. When it stopped, he saw his daughter exit and the driver follow her to the door with shopping bags in hand. Philippe briskly made his way to the foyer but discovered his daughter in a sprint to the staircase.

"Jolene!" He caught her attention, and she halted, flashing him an annoyed glance. "Might I have a word with you?"

"Can this wait until later?" she pleaded, taking another step.

Philippe scowled and reached out and grabbed her arm. "No, it cannot. I would appreciate you following me to the library for a private conversation."

Jolene glanced at the driver who stood like a statue with bags hanging from both his hands. "You can leave them here," Jolene instructed. "I'll have one of the maids bring them upstairs." The driver set the bags along the wall, tipped his hat, and retreated.

As Philippe made his way down the hallway to the library, he sucked in a deep breath to control his bout of anger toward his daughter. They had not argued about anything since they were reunited, but now he could not be silent. For the sake of Suzette and his concern, cautionary words were in order.

"Why don't you have a seat," he said, pointing to a nearby chair. Philippe closed the door for privacy. He chose a chair across from Jolene, whose eyes darted around the room avoiding eye contact. "Look at me," he softly implored. "Might I ask why you felt it necessary to leave without telling anyone except the butler you were off to London?"

Jolene fiddled with her skirt. After a few moments, she finally lifted her eyes and observed him warily. "I had things to do and didn't want to bother anyone."

"Shopping?" Philippe frowned. "If that were the case, then why didn't you invite your mother to come with you?" Jolene suddenly blushed, which Philippe knew to be a rarity. She pulled her eyes away and sighed. Her actions caused Philippe to release a lighthearted chuckle.

"Why are you laughing?" Jolene scowled.

"After eighteen years of not having you with me, I am after one year together able to tell when you stretch the truth." He shook his head. "You get a little twitch above your left eyebrow as if it's complaining about the explicit fib exiting your mouth."

She narrowed her eyes at him showing her displeasure. "Honestly, Father, there are times I find you exasperating."

He was right. "So where were you?" Philippe lost his smile. He wanted the truth of her whereabouts.

"I met Viscount Derrington for lunch at the Savoy Hotel and then went to the Whitefields to apologize to Alastair for my behavior."

"Hmm," Philippe murmured, restraining his disappointment. "You met a stranger unescorted." His eyes narrowed, showing his displeasure.

"Well, it was in a public place. I did have the sense to arrange that much," Jolene said. She adjusted her posture as if to draw a defensive line.

"Who is this viscount? Is he asking to court you?" Philippe leaned forward attempting to rein in his instinctive protectiveness.

"He has asked me to attend the opera with him," Jolene began. "I find him to be a very pleasant individual."

"What do you know about him?"

Jolene lowered her head and bit her lower lip. "Not very much, except that he is from York and is in London on business."

Philippe pondered the lack of good sense his daughter displayed. Clearly, she was smitten by the man evidenced by the dreamy expression in her eyes as she talked about him. *Young love*, he thought. It could be a dangerous thing to a woman who never experienced the undivided attention of a man who attracted her emotionally or physically. Suddenly he wanted to call in Suzette to take over the conversation giving their daughter advice. But a painful memory of her indiscretion at a young age cautioned his heart, and he wondered if he would ever get over the past.

"I don't like it," he snapped. "If you are interested in this man, then do not sneak about trying to hide it from your family." He rose to his feet distressed. "In fact, if he were any kind of gentleman, he would ask to meet your family and speak to me of his intentions before even suggesting you meet alone."

"Your notions are archaic," Jolene complained. "This is 1908, Father, not 1808. Things have changed. Women can make their own decisions without parental consent when choosing a spouse."

Shocked at her outburst, Philippe's jaw dropped. His gaze bore into his daughter's eyes, and he saw one thing—his own stubbornness and pride staring back at him. Apparently, she inherited her gumption from his blood, and now he was faced with the unpleasant task of dealing with it.

"Honestly, Jolene, I do not believe that you are thinking wisely. Why would you even consider pursuing a relationship with someone who lives in northern England? Have you forgotten you are a komtesse with an estate back in Vienna?"

"Attending the opera with him is not the same as a marriage ceremony," she said indifferently. "I enjoy his company. He makes me feel…"

"Feel what?" Philippe sucked in a breath leery of her reply.

Jolene turned away and put a few feet of distance between them. She avoided his gaze, and Philippe feared the gentleman had been the first to stir within her the sense of physical attraction. The little baby he once held in his arms was indeed a young woman on the brink of entering into a part of life she knew nothing about. The lure could pull her into a place where her mother once failed to resist. Philippe didn't know what to do or say to convince her to use good judgment rather than emotions.

"I forbid you to see him again." The words flew from between his lips without restraint, laced with fear and authority. Jolene swung around and glared at him angrily.

"You forbid me? How dare you!" She took an aggressive step toward him and bellowed in response. "You will not tell me what I can and cannot do in life. I am of age, an heiress, and titled komtesse—not some baby you lost eighteen years ago."

As she glowered at him, a knock came at the door. A second

later it opened slightly to reveal Suzette.

"Is everything all right?" she asked with a worried glint in her eyes. "I heard loud voices."

Seeing his ex-wife inflamed the painful memories of eighteen years ago. Suzette was a perfect example of a woman drawn by temptation and seduced by a man.

"I'm done here," he grumbled, pushing brusquely past Suzette. "Perhaps you can put some sense into your daughter's head drawing from your experience. She apparently doesn't want my wisdom in the matter."

He stomped down the hall and flew out the front entrance of the estate to get a breath of fresh air.

"She's bullheaded, independent, and a naïve woman who knows nothing about life," he spewed in private.

How could he protect her when he failed to do so the day she had been kidnapped? Her return brought joy after so many years of sadness. It literally ached in his chest to think he could lose her again and be helpless to prevent its reoccurrence. Hopefully, Suzette would caution her about nurturing an infatuation with a total stranger.

Suzette struggled the entire day with the pain of rejection, having heard that Jolene left for London alone to go shopping. Ever since her daughter arrived, they barely spent any time together. Jolene's calendar had been filled with activities, leaving little opportunity for discussions between a mother and daughter. Mealtime seemed to be the only free time they had to speak, which revolved around superficial chitchat with others at the table.

It appeared that not only her relationship suffered but also Philippe's, as she heard them arguing on the other side of the library door. Curious, she halted to listen.

Suzette brought her hand to her mouth astonished at the brash and rude responses Jolene screamed at her father. Perhaps she should have waited to hear Philippe's response to his daughter's outburst, but she could not. She opened the door and peeked inside. Even though Philippe's back was to her when she entered, she could easily tell by the clench fists at his side that he was not pleased. After inquiring, Philippe bolted past her mumbling incoherently about talking sense into Jolene.

Now that they were together alone in the same room, Suzette witnessed Jolene's red face and bulging veins in her neck.

"Why don't you sit down," Suzette cajoled, stepping toward her. "Take a deep breath until your wrath dissipates."

Jolene stiffened defensively, but Suzette tilted her head and with a warm smile gave her motherly encouragement. Eventually her daughter relented and lowered herself onto a wingbacked chair.

"Now, tell me what you were arguing about with your father," she said, reaching out and touching Jolene's hand. "All that anger makes your beautiful face look out of sorts."

"Out of sorts," Jolene repeated. "Yes, I'm sure it does. Father can be so exasperating!"

Suzette pulled her hand away and sat down in a chair. "Your voice carried out the door, but I only heard enough to ascertain he was giving you advice you did not wish to heed."

"Forbid was the term he used. Does he think he can forbid me to do anything?" she heaved. Her angry countenance swiftly returned.

"Do you want to talk about it?" Suzette warily inquired. Her daughter remained still, inhaling deep breaths to calm her fury.

"I'm sorry," she began, lifting her gaze, "for not inviting you to come shopping with me."

Suzette shrugged her shoulders and shook her head in understanding. "No worries," she replied halfheartedly. "I'm sure you had your reasons." She did not wish to risk their fragile relationship by causing discontent about a shopping spree, so she kept the offense hidden.

"I had lunch with a man," Jolene announced nonchalantly.

It proved difficult not to comment about her daughter's indiscretion, but she held her tongue. Jolene's admission revealed Philippe's apparent response to that tidbit of news. Recalling his parting statement made sense about drawing from her own experience. Understanding the meaning behind his brash comment confirmed that being forgiven did not mean forgotten.

With great difficulty she summoned her own inner strength and suppressed her lower lip wanting to quiver over the wounding words. She needed to turn away from the past and focus upon Jolene, who sat awaiting her response.

"I see," she began, nodding her head. "That explains your father's reaction."

"I could not reason with him at all! He just puffed out his chest like a bear, forbidding me to see the viscount again."

"The viscount?" Suzette stirred her memory over the morning breakfast when he was first mentioned. "You mean the man who rescued you from Geoffrey at the ball?" A slow smile curled the corner of her daughter's lips. Suddenly her eyes brightened.

"Yes, that's him."

"I assumed the two of you had parted afterward, as there had been no mention of seeing him again." Suzette pondered the next argument that would undoubtedly ensue with her half brother over the matter.

"Well, we corresponded by letter and decided to meet again," Jolene responded. She averted her gaze toward Suzette, which gave rise to further suspicion.

"So I take it you met, and I'm assuming you had a pleasant time and wish to see him again." Her actions were definitely not a wise decision, which apparently ignited Philippe's harsh reprisal.

"Yes, he's invited me to the opera, and I do wish to accept. He even suggested I bring someone with me if I felt uncomfortable or my family objected."

"You realize, of course, being seen in public with a man to whom you are not married is considered scandalous behavior in English society." Suzette could tell her daughter had every intention of going even if her father forbade it or society frowned. As far as her own thoughts on the matter, she had the distinct impression her daughter would only chafe against any advice.

"I do not care what people think," Jolene replied.

"Do you find him to be a pleasant person?" she asked out of curiosity.

"Oh yes, very much so," Jolene grinned.

The sparkle in her eye spoke of much more than pleasantry, and Suzette realized Jolene was embarking into unchartered territory of womanhood.

"You are attracted to him," she said matter-of-factly. "He is the first to catch your eye in such a way, isn't he?" Suzette gave her a warm smile rather than a stern frown of disapproval. Jolene lowered her head and grinned sheepishly.

"Well, yes, I find him attractive in appearance."

"That's not what I meant," Suzette clarified firmly. "I mean sexually attracted to him as a woman is to a man. By the sparkle in your eye, young lady, I think you had more than lunch together."

Jolene's eyes widened. "Are you insinuating he had bedded me already?"

Suzette chuckled. "Well, if he has, I would say after two meetings that would qualify as very roguish behavior."

Her comment made Jolene giggle. "He kissed me in the garden at the masquerade," she admitted.

"Oh, a kiss under the stars—how very romantic for a young lady," she replied. "I'm assuming your knees grew weak, your flesh tingled, and you could barely speak or think afterward." A growing smile lifted Jolene's lips as if she were thankful that finally someone understood her current state of mind.

"Is that how you felt with the duke the first time he kissed you?"

"Oh dear," Suzette said, thinking of the brothel and the scene from so long ago. "All I remember is his tenderness, but frankly, I was so petrified thinking he would take my virginity my fear outweighed any sense of attraction."

"If not then, surely you did later," Jolene said. She earnestly waited for confirmation.

"Yes, of course I did. He bewitched me with his tenderness. It did not take long for desire to consume me to such an extent I gave myself to him without a second thought." Suzette lowered her head worried that her statement would give Jolene the wrong impression. She did not wish to convey her permission to let herself go, as she had done with Robert so many times as his mistress and during their affair. Robert enticed her in a way she could not resist. Even after all the years together, she continued to feel helpless whenever he became the aggressive lover.

"Bewitched is an interesting word to use," Jolene commented thoughtfully. "That seems to imply you were helpless to resist."

"I made many poor choices in my youth, though some of them were pressed upon me out of desperation. Nevertheless, I loved Robert, and yes I was helpless to resist him in many ways to the point of becoming an adulteress while married to your father." The confession of her sin to her daughter was grievous, but she wanted to make a point of what uncontrollable lust could do to a young lady. "Don't underestimate the power of passion, Jolene. You may think you are strong enough to resist, but pride always comes before the fall."

"Is that what you think of me, a woman puffed up with so much pride that I will not be able to control myself?" Jolene's anger returned, and now the glowering glare she had given her father rested upon Suzette.

"I think this is your first encounter with physical attraction toward a man," Suzette clarified. "You may believe yourself to be a strong Austrian komtesse, but do not forget in your veins flow the blood of the French."

"For God's sake," Jolene replied, jumping to her feet. "All I want to do is go to the opera with the man." She brushed passed Suzette's chair and headed for the door. "I'm going to accept his invitation with or without anyone's blessing."

Suzette rose and called after her. "Wait," she cried.

Her daughter halted and slowly turned around. "You are my darling daughter, and I only wish to counsel you from my experience. I believe that is what your father inferred as he stormed from the room."

"I will heed your advice," Jolene replied, lowering her eyes. "But I promise you and father nothing further."

Jolene left Suzette alone, feeling dreadful that perhaps she handled the matter poorly. She felt no reassurance her daughter would heed anything. So many years apart from one another had given them no time to form a loving and trustful relationship.

Suzette frowned as disappointment threatened tears.

Her daughter turned out nothing like her. The meekness of her personality had not tempered her one bit. Instead, Jolene's personality closely mirrored Philippe—stubborn and prideful. Since both of them failed to counsel her, Suzette knew of only one other person who could possibly do otherwise. It was time to elicit the help of her son.

CHAPTER 13

"*La Bohème*," he said, finding Jolene at her writing desk. He surmised she was penning a letter to the viscount to accept his invitation to the opera Friday evening. If there was anything Robert knew firsthand, it was that when parents forbade their children to do anything, it only made them more defiant. Since his half sister no doubt shared his rebellious streak, it would take diplomacy to rectify the current situation as described to him by his mother. Jolene glanced up at him peering down at the paper, which she quickly flipped over.

"What about it?" She looked up at him curiously.

"I have been told that you wish Grace and me to attend the performance along with you and this stranger." Robert paused and stroked his chin with a mischievous smile. "What's his name again?"

"James Derrington." She smirked.

"Is that James Robert Derrington, James Dudley Derrington, James Giles Derrington, James—"

"Oh, now you are teasing me. I don't know his middle name," she said, looking down at the desktop.

"Well, finish your note to the man and let him know that we will meet him at the opera house thirty minutes before the performance. We can use the family box," he added.

"Father talked to you, no doubt," she said, making a disgruntled face.

"And Mother too. In the short time that you have been here, you have already caused a stir amongst the household."

Jolene rose from the chair and frowned at him. "I suppose you will be the family chaperone," she said, pulling her mouth to one side to show her disapproval.

"No, I will be your sibling, looking out for your best interests."

"Well, all right, then," Jolene sighed. She sat back down behind the writing desk and flipped over the paper. "I will let him know the arrangements."

"Will he mind?" Robert looked suspiciously at Jolene.

"No, in fact, he suggested that if my family felt uncomfortable, he more than welcomed someone else attend."

"Well, if that's the case, he has obtained his first favorable point for being a gentleman," Robert jested.

"Oh, I can see it now," Jolene said. "You will be running a tally of good and bad points and then reporting back to Father and Mother regarding your expert opinion of the man."

"Do you think me that devious?" Robert countered. Actually, he had already planned his strategy. Rather than having Jolene consort with a man she hardly knew, he would make sure that the viscount would be placed front and center of the entire family. Being under scrutiny would solve two problems—Jolene spending time with him alone and the family's opportunity to discover the man's character.

"Let me give you a piece of advice," Robert said.

Jolene rolled her eyes. "I have been showered with advice by others so you might as well join in."

"If you wish for this man to find acceptance, then you need to openly include him into family affairs."

"What do you mean?"

"Stop sneaking around behind everyone's back with clandestine meetings. It only appears as if you wish to hide your behavior with him." Robert saw her brow crease as if she were digesting the wisdom of his suggestion. "Place your relationship with him in the center of everyone who holds you dear so others may assess his worthiness of your attention."

"Why must he be judged?"

"Because you are loved, and no one wishes to see you hurt." Robert smiled warmly, hoping she would relent.

"Well, I suppose you do have a point," she admitted, pouting as if it pained her to agree.

"A wise choice." Robert gave her a brotherly peck on the cheek. "Write your note to your prince charming, sweet princess, that we shall accompany you to the opera." He flashed a wink and headed for the door. As he reached the threshold, Jolene called after him.

"You are a rascal!"

"Indeed," he drawled, inwardly gloating at his ability to sway a stubborn woman.

Jolene stood in the foyer of London's Royal Opera House. At her side were Grace and Robert awaiting the arrival of James. She knew that Robert had her best interest at heart but also worried that the poor man would be subject to intense scrutiny the entire evening. If he did not pass Robert's approval, surely she would be faced with the decision to scandalously pursue the relationship. Undoubtedly, Robert and Grace would evaluate his qualities against those of Alastair's. Jolene admitted she was hard-pressed to find anything negative about Grace's brother, who professed his love for her a few days ago.

While nervously clutching her small reticule, she caught a glimpse of another group of patrons arriving through the entrance. Unable to control the slightest hint of excitement, a broad smile spread across her face when she spotted James. As he caught her eye and began approaching, she admired the way that he carried himself with dignity. His tall stature and broad shoulders accented the authority of his appearance, exuding a muscular frame beneath his formal evening attire.

"He's here," she blurted to Robert and Grace.

"I have no doubt by your exuberant announcement," Robert teased.

Jolene closed her eyes and inhaled a deep breath to calm her jitters. As she opened them, he stood only a few feet away, looking at her with admiration.

"Komtesse," he said, bowing at the waist. "It is a pleasure to see you again."

"Viscount." She lifted her hand, and he took advantage of her offer and pressed a kiss against her trembling fingers. Jolene felt helpless to suppress the broad smile and flush of her cheeks. She pulled her hand away and turned her attention to Robert, who suspiciously glanced up and down at James.

"May I introduce you to my half brother, Lord Holland, and his fiancée, Lady Whitefield." She turned toward Robert. "Viscount Derrington," Jolene announced.

"It is a pleasure to make your acquaintance." James nodded respectfully to both Robert and Grace.

"Indeed," Robert responded with an air of snobbery. "We are pleased to make your acquaintance as well. Jolene has spoken of her fondness for your company."

"Robert," Jolene protested, shooting him an irritated glance.

"I am not ashamed to admit that I am fond of her company as well." He offered her his arm. "She is a charming and intelligent woman."

She glanced at Grace, who remained quietly by Robert's side, displaying a rather cold demeanor. Undoubtedly, she still nurtured resentment at the spurning of her brother's affections.

"Robert, will you be so kind as to lead us to your family's box?" Jolene asked.

"Of course." He escorted Grace, and they followed behind.

"It is good to see you again," James said in a low tone. He gave her arm a slight squeeze. "You look absolutely stunning this evening."

His flattery made her heart race, along with the tingling attraction of his touch. Jolene found him impossible to resist, and an overwhelming sense of peace flooded her soul.

"Thank you." The struggle to keep her emotions in check would be a challenge the entire evening.

As they entered the box, Grace sat to the left of Robert. James chose to sit to the right of Robert, and she took the chair to the right of James. It appeared that he purposely placed himself near her half brother to give him an opportunity to talk more freely with him. She uttered a silent plea to heaven that he would succeed in making a good impression.

Jolene flipped open the program handed to her as they entered and began perusing the cast. It did not take very long for Robert to begin his interrogation as she heard him strike up a conversation with James.

"Thank you for joining us this evening," he said. "It places Jolene in a much better situation socially to be in your company alongside her family, don't you agree?"

She noticed James's jaw tighten as she glanced at him for his reaction to Robert's comment. Obviously, Robert had made a point to express his displeasure about their secret meeting only a few days beforehand. Jolene hoped that James would give a genteel response, even though she feared he found the comment offensive.

"I have the komtesse's best interests at heart," he coolly but calmly stated. "You can be assured that it is not my intention to harm her reputation."

"I am relieved to hear of it."

Robert eyed him suspiciously, and Jolene cringed. *Oh, Robert, please do not embarrass me*, she cried inwardly. To her surprise, James did not reply to Robert's threatening tone. Instead, he turned his head toward her and looked into her eyes.

"I have no intention of harming your reputation," he assured her.

"Frankly, I am confident that your intentions are nothing but honorable," Jolene positively confirmed. She purposely spoke the words loud enough for Robert to take heed. Jolene did trust James, but she wondered if she could trust herself. The closeness of his body next to hers aroused an alluring attraction. As she wrestled with the overwhelming urges surging through her body, the lights dimmed. Thankfully, the curtain opened, and Jolene took the opportunity to place her mind elsewhere.

Her hand clutched the program until it wrinkled between her fingers. After a sharp inhale of breath to calm her nerves, she released her grip and fixed her mind on the stage. The music rose in crescendos, but Jolene sensed the nearness of James challenging her attention. A moment later she felt his hand rest upon her own that fidgeted in her lap. She turned to acknowledge his touch, but he appeared engrossed in the production, not returning her glance. Nevertheless, a slight smile curled the corner of his mouth acknowledging his awareness of her emotion. He touched her hand tenderly and swiftly withdrew it. James's reassurance quieted her butterflies. Jolene lost herself amongst the voices, costumes, and story.

–·✳·–

Robert struggled with an uneasy feeling throughout the entire evening. With Grace to his left, the viscount to his right, and Jolene nearby gave him no time to enjoy the opera. Not that he cared for the entertainment, but it would have been welcome had it been successful in taking his mind elsewhere from the worrisome, gnawing thoughts rumbling around in his head.

His complicated emotions confirmed that he had become extremely fond of Jolene, so much to the point that he wanted to protect her from harm. Nevertheless, he had to admit that she deserved happiness as much as any other person did their age. No doubt she wished to marry and have children, which was probably why she felt drawn to the viscount. The entire affair would have been much easier had she succumbed to Alastair's wooing instead. However, he knew from the onset that the odds were stacked against his friend in spite of his irreproachable character.

As far as this new chap was concerned, Robert hated being in the dark regarding the man's background. Title or not, he could be a rake of the lowest sort. The thought caused Robert's nostrils to flare as he pictured the man taking advantage of Jolene.

When the curtain finally fell, Robert rose to his feet with the crowd and gave his usual bravos with the other attendees. The lights illuminated the auditorium, and his eyes glanced at the seats in orchestra stalls. To his surprise, he saw Geoffrey rise to his feet, with an unrecognizable young lady at his side.

"Oh, bloody hell," he mumbled loud enough for Grace to catch his curse.

"What's the matter?"

"Geoffrey Chambers," he said faintly, hoping Jolene would not hear. "In the orchestra stalls."

As soon as the words left his lips, Geoffrey lifted his head to their family box, and a bright smile spread across his face. He nodded at Robert, and he noticed his eyes glance over at Jolene. As soon as he saw the viscount, his smile faded.

"We should go," Robert announced.

"James, would that be agreeable?" Jolene asked with anticipation.

"Yes, I see no reason why not." He offered her his arm.

Robert did not hesitate to leave the box and make his way down the stairs heading for a side exit rather than the main doors.

"I know a quicker way out of here," he announced, sprinting in the direction.

"Why the rush?" Jolene called after him.

Robert continued to trot down the staircase without answering.

"Tell her before she breaks a leg running out the door," Grace said out of breath.

"Geoffrey. Need I saw more?"

"Oh, dear God," Jolene gasped. "Say no more."

James remained quiet and unconcerned until Robert burst open the double doors and they found themselves out in the cool of the night. Other patrons milled about the sidewalks while Robert's eyes scanned the area relieved that Geoffrey had been lost in the crowd.

"Is there something that I should be concerned about?" he questioned.

"No, nothing," Jolene assured him.

"My driver is waiting just down at the corner," Robert directed. "Why don't we get a bite to eat?"

"My sincerest apologies," James suddenly announced. "Unfortunately, I must be elsewhere later this evening, regarding a private matter."

"You must leave?" Jolene inquired with a disappointing glance. James took her hand and lifted it to his lips, giving it a tender kiss.

Robert wrinkled his brow over his declaration. "Well, if you must go, then by all means tend to your private matters," he curtly countered.

"Komtesse, it was indeed a pleasure to see you." He turned toward Robert. "And I am most happy to have made your acquaintance, Lord Holland, and that of your lovely companion."

He tipped his hat and gazed affectionately at Jolene. "Until we meet again."

Robert merely nodded, keeping his lips in a straight line of disapproval. The horrified expression on Jolene's face screamed her disappointment. He could not quite understand the man's abrupt departure either.

"Well, that action was an unexpected occurrence," Grace mumbled. "Are you all right, Jolene?"

"I am fine, thank you." She turned her attention to Grace and Robert after James disappeared into the crowd. "He must have his reasons," she added, forcing a fake grin. "Robert, I am starving. Does your offer for dinner still stand?"

"Of course it does. Two beautiful women on either side of me. What more could a man want?"

He offered his elbow to each. Robert's eyes glanced about the dissipating crowd as he led Jolene and Grace to their waiting motorcar. Alastair would enjoy hearing this tidbit about their night out and wondered what, if anything, he would conclude regarding the viscount's strange behavior.

CHAPTER 14

"You mean to tell me that he just left her without an explanation?" Alastair asked, pacing back and forth at an annoying speed.

"Well, he gave an explanation of personal business of some sort but did not elaborate." Robert's eyes blurred watching his friend's antics.

"What do you make of it?" Alastair halted his step in front of Robert. "For that matter, what do you think of him?"

"Sit down, Alastair. Your nervous marching is irritating. Take a drink and relax." Robert pointed at a nearby empty chair, giving his friend a commanding stare.

"Fine." After lowering himself on the seat cushion, he continued. "So as I inquired earlier, what do you make of it or him or whatever?"

"We barely spoke, frankly. I think Jolene blames me for scaring him off." Robert chuckled. "I did make one snide remark regarding his intentions."

"Well done on that point," Alastair agreed. "Has he made an attempt to contact her again?"

"Not that I know of," Robert replied. "Probably for the best." Alastair's distraught expression relaxed. "Now don't go getting your hopes up. He could very well be back."

"True, but you must admit his behavior is quite odd," Alastair mused, narrowing his eyes at the mystery. Afterward, he admitted his devious actions. "You know, I hired a private detective to investigate him further."

"You did what?" Robert leaned forward in his chair.

"You heard me."

"And have you discovered anything out of the ordinary?"

"Nothing yet. Inquiries are being made around York about his family."

Robert roared with laughter.

"What's so bloody humorous?" Alastair scowled.

"Well, I'm afraid then you have uncovered nothing more than my investigator."

"I'll be damned, Holland, you too?"

"Well, what do you expect? You may be in love with her, but I'm obligated to care for her well-being as her sibling," Robert justified. A conniving grin lifted the corner of his mouth. "I suppose there is no reason to pay for two investigators. Why don't I cancel my inquiry and you can continue on your own?"

Alastair shook his head. "So the expense comes from my pocket instead?"

"The arrangement makes perfect sense to me," Robert snorted.

"You never cease to amaze me," Alastair moaned. He fell silent and then turned his concerns elsewhere. "Not to change the subject, but when are you planning on marrying my sister? Grace tells me you have yet to set a date."

"A date?" Robert paled. "I have not proposed!"

"Oh, don't tell me you have cold feet, Holland." Alastair snickered.

After shifting uncomfortably in his chair, Robert chafed at the unexpected inquiry. He and Grace were getting along splendidly, and he did not want to rush his walk down the aisle. No matter how much he loved her, a man needed to prepare for marriage. A part of his wild and rakish heart had to mourn the fact that he would no longer enjoy other beautiful ladies that caught his eye. Also, he reflected upon the looming possibility of becoming a father in the very near future. The possibility frightened the daylights out of him.

Alastair, sensing his hesitation, scowled. "If you have an

inclination about breaking my sister's heart, I'll break your bloody nose."

"Now see here," Robert protested. "I intend to keep my nose in one piece so unclench your fist."

"Why are you hesitating then? Get on your knee, set a date, and marry her." Alastair rolled his eyes. "Besides, she keeps talking wedding dresses with Mother, but I see on her face the disappointment of your foot-dragging toward the altar."

Robert's caddish grin faded. His friend was quite right. As much as he hated to admit it, perhaps he had been toying with Grace's patience far too long.

"I agree," he sighed in resignation. "Perhaps it is time to set a date in the next three to six months."

"Well, get a ring and propose first, you sod," Alastair responded. He rose to his feet and walked over to a decanter of brandy on the side table. "Need a drink?" he asked, with a cockeyed smile.

"Better make it a double," Robert bantered.

Alastair poured an ample amount into Robert's glass. "Too bad that we cannot make it a double wedding. I would have liked it," he pensively mused. His countenance saddened.

"Now would you?" Robert uttered amusingly with an arched brow.

"So much for wishful thinking," Alastair sighed, handing the glass to Robert. "Let's toast to your upcoming nuptials instead, my friend."

"If you insist." Robert raised his glass with Alastair.

"To my loyal friend and soon to be brother-in-law, I cannot think of anyone else worthy to marry and care for my sister."

Alastair's affectionate toast moved Robert and brought chills down his spine. Jolene's inability to see the goodness in his friend discouraged him.

"Here is hoping that the viscount whatever-his-name-is will not return," Robert said. "Perhaps you'll have another chance with Jolene."

"Perhaps," Alastair replied.

They tipped their glasses and drank to their futures.

-·⁂·-

Robert checked for the third time, making sure that the diamond ring he had chosen for Grace remained hidden in his vest pocket. His hand trembled, and the lump in his throat felt like a hard apple. He had not realized that proposing would take such a mental toll upon his bachelor psyche. Nevertheless it had, and outwardly he appeared a nervous wreck.

"Come on, Holland," he scolded himself, taking a last glance in the mirror. "Get ahold of yourself. She wants to marry a confident gentleman, not a bumbling idiot." A little voice whispered in his ear. "She's going to turn you down."

"Turn me down?" he answered the taunting thought. To be frank, Robert had not considered such an outcome. Grace loved him and hinted at marriage constantly. He thought for a second and frowned. "I've waited too long. She will say no just to punish me for doing so."

After inhaling a shaky breath, Robert trotted downstairs to the waiting car. He caught sight of his mother and father standing in the foyer.

"About time you decided to settle down," his father said. He grabbed Robert's hand and gave him a hearty pat on the upper arm.

"Don't tease him." Suzette chuckled. "Though I must admit it will be wonderful having Grace a member of the family."

"You haven't informed Jolene or Philippe of my intentions, have you?"

"No," his father answered. "We wanted the news to come directly from you when you announce the engagement."

"Good then." Robert pulled at his waistcoat and fiddled with the rim of his hat.

"The car is waiting, your lordship," the footman announced.

"Well, I am off." He turned and headed for the door.

"You do have the ring, right?" his mother called after him.

Robert halted and patted his waistcoat pocket. "Yes, safe and sound next to my heart. I couldn't think of a better place to keep it." A broad smile spread across his mother's face, and Robert gave her an affectionate wink in return.

"Good luck, son." Robert nodded at his father and stepped out-of-doors.

He planned the event entirely on his own accord. A casual dinner at a small restaurant he fancied near Trafalgar Square would set the cadence. Robert wanted a relaxing few hours together to chat and calm himself. A few glasses of champagne might help him reach a place of confidence, but he also did not want to overindulge in food or drink. Such combinations made him less than a gentleman.

The car slowed and stopped at the Whitefield's residence. As the driver opened the door, he reiterated his plans.

"Drop us off at the restaurant and then return for us in front of Buckingham Palace at around ten o'clock," he instructed. "Please repeat nothing of what I've told you in front of Lady Whitefield."

The driver nodded in agreement. "As you wish."

Robert turned and walked toward the door, giving the knocker a few raps. It swung open to reveal Alastair on the other side. His friend had no idea of his planned evening but wondered if he suspected.

"I don't know if I will let you take Grace out this evening," he said, smirking at him. Alastair stood centered in the doorway, placing both hands on either side of the doorframe. While he stood smugly blocking Robert's entrance, Grace swiftly slipped through underneath his arms, escaping her would-be jailer.

"Sorry, Alastair, but you know the rules." She grabbed Robert's hand. "No teasing allowed."

"Then what amusement am I to have in life?" he moaned, crossing his arms in front of his body.

"Well, you could become more social and look for a woman to keep you company," Robert said as he led Grace to the car.

"You are quite comical," Alastair replied. He stepped back into the foyer and shut the door with a bang.

"You're a tease too," Grace scolded. "You know very well his heart is languishing over Jolene."

As they settled into the car and the driver pulled away, Robert reached over and took Grace's hand.

"Good gracious, Robert, your fingers are as cold as ice. Are you all right?" She tilted her head and looked at him with concern. "Are you getting a fever?"

She went to place her free hand on his forehead when he pulled away. "No, I'm not ill," he assured her. "Just tired, I guess. Perhaps my heart isn't pumping enough blood to my extremities." It sounded plausible to Robert.

"Well, then," Grace drawled teasingly, "I know quite a few ways to get your heart to pump faster." She trailed her finger along his lower lip, flashing him a wicked grin.

"Don't get me started in the backseat of this car," he said. "The driver will think I'm a scoundrel if I start warming my hands in certain places on your body."

Grace snickered. After they had settled back into their seats, Robert kept his focus on the upcoming dinner hour. It would be a long night of anticipation and nerves.

CHAPTER 15

Robert and Suzette kept their promise and did not raise any conversations regarding their son's impending engagement. As they sat at the dining table with Philippe and Jolene taking supper, Suzette sensed a troublesome mood hovering in the atmosphere.

Jolene's morose countenance displayed her disappointment about the absence of another invitation from her admirer. Robert told her of the evening's outcome, relaying his sudden departure after the opera. Her daughter must have been deeply hurt about his questioning exodus. The more Suzette thought about the occurrence, the more she doubted his sincerity. Perhaps he decided to turn his attentions to another lady with an English background. After all, Jolene would eventually return to Vienna. What future could they hope to have together?

The other troubled soul in the room sat to her right. Her husband had been quiet and distant the entire day, which caused concern. It made no sense to inquire about what weighed on his mind because he would never tell her. He was not a man to share his burdens with anyone. Nevertheless, something had been troubling him. Even his actions at the dining room table revealed his unease. Robert pushed his food around in circles rather than eating much of anything.

"Have you no appetite?" she asked. Suzette glanced at his silver fork stabbing his potatoes.

"My appetite is fine," he replied, obviously lying. Trying to prove his point, he took a bite.

"You seem distracted and lost in your vegetables, but I understand you probably have things on your mind."

Philippe glanced at Robert and Suzette. His curious gaze caught Suzette's eyes.

"Anything I can do?" he offered.

"Probably cheer up your daughter," Robert replied.

Suzette thought his comment crude. She glanced at Jolene and saw her perturbed unease.

"Well, that was not helpful," Suzette whispered in her husband's ear. She wanted to poke Robert but restrained herself.

In an attempt to fix the damage of Robert's untimely comment, Philippe leaned toward Jolene and spoke. "It's only been three days. The viscount said he came to London to attend to business, did he not?"

"Yes, he did," Jolene said.

"After he concludes his private affairs, perhaps you will receive another invitation to dinner or the opera."

Philippe's comforting voice seemed to ease Jolene's countenance somewhat, but Suzette surmised Philippe had other motives as an overprotective parent.

"Maybe we should send him an invitation to a dinner party here at the estate," Suzette suggested. Robert's head swiftly twisted in her direction.

"A what?"

"A dinner party," she reiterated. "You know, a small gathering of close friends who come for dinner, drinks, and an evening of entertainment. Sending him an invitation to a mere social function would cause no harm."

Robert smirked. "Simple? If I know you, it shall be extravagant and expensive."

"Brilliant idea," Philippe interjected. "It would serve as a proper environment."

Suzette thought it might make an excellent engagement party too, but held her tongue. As she returned to nibble at her food, her thoughts turned to her son, and she wondered how he fared with his proposal. Hopefully, for Grace's sake, it would be a memorable occasion rather than a swift and unromantic affair. Her whimsical thinking was naturally due to her romantic notions.

"Jolene, I will pen an invitation and have it sent by courier to his hotel," Suzette announced. "You do know where he is staying, correct?"

"Yes, of course," Jolene answered, smiling with excitement. "He is rooming at the Savoy."

"Well, he must have money if he's staying there for a period of time," Suzette responded. "What do you know about his family?"

"His family?" Jolene gulped. "Well, very little actually." She fiddled with her napkin as if she were embarrassed over how little she knew. "He has not conveyed anything to me about his family or home in York."

Philippe chortled a response. "Jolene, remember that you are Austrian with French blood. Our ways are not the ways of the English, who look quite differently on such matters." He glanced over at the duke, waiting for a reaction.

"Your father is quite right," the duke agreed. Suddenly his sullen mood vanished when he spoke of the habits of proper English society. "It's considered a gross impertinence to make inquiry of personal affairs from a person of whom you know little about. When and if the man is ready for such private conversation, he may see fit to share details regarding his parentage."

Suzette could not help but burst out laughing. "You see, my darling daughter, it doesn't matter what you do not know about the man. In English society, it really matters that you know nothing. It is better to remain silent than to be thought vulgar."

Philippe and Suzette shared a knowing glance with each other. With fondness, she remembered their youth and the freedom they shared. The French were more vocal and unreserved, unlike her husband who tenaciously clung to his traditions.

"Where is Robert this evening?" Jolene inquired.

"Out with Grace, I believe." Suzette avoided eye contact when answering the question, not wishing to relay a glint in her eye of his plans.

"He has good taste," Philippe added. "Even her name Grace agrees with her elegance, beauty, and poise."

"I adore Grace," Jolene added. "She is kind, polite, and thoughtful, much like her brother Alastair."

A slight tremble in Jolene's voice betrayed a hint of remorse, which surprised Suzette. Before she could think further of it, Robert spoke.

"Philippe, would you mind joining me in my study for a cigar and brandy?"

"That depends on the types of cigars," he said, snickering. "You do know I used to sell them and am well acquainted with the best of brands."

"Smoke what I have, and if you do not agree with their quality, I will welcome your recommendations."

"Agreed," Philippe replied.

"Ladies, you may sit and talk about eligible bachelors over tea," Robert said. He rose from his chair and nodded at Philippe, who had completed his meal. "Shall we?"

Philippe dabbed his lips with his napkin and pushed back his chair. "Ladies," he said, nodding at Suzette and Jolene.

"Enjoy your manly pursuits," Suzette replied. After they had departed the room, Suzette turned to Jolene. "Well now, what frivolous conversations shall we pursue?"

"Would you mind terribly if we had another glass of wine in the parlor rather than tea?" Jolene smirked mischievously.

"Not at all." Suzette reached out, touched her daughter's arm, and gave it a slight pat. "Why don't we just be ill-mannered and have two."

— ·�֍· —

Robert had been dreading the conversation for days. Words swirled around in his mind as he tried to formulate what he needed to say. He wanted a drink and a stiff one.

"Here's your brandy," he said, handing Philippe a glass. Robert proceeded to the cigar box on the corner of his desk. He flipped open the lid and presented the open case to Philippe.

"For your perusal," he offered.

"Not bad at all," Philippe replied. After surveying the contents, he reached out and picked up a cigar. "You have good taste, sir."

Robert chose one as well, and after they lit and settled into their chairs, he decided to face the inevitable.

"You know," he began, taking a few puffs. "Since we have come to know one another, I have grown to respect you as a man." He felt no embarrassment over his confession. Years ago, he loathed him.

"Considering our past," Philippe said, "I am somewhat surprised."

"Yes, we have a rather complicated history, but it is the future that I wish to bring into the conversation now." Robert repositioned himself in his seat and noted his former nemesis staring at him curiously. One brow arched above his left eye, which he noticed to be a quirky habit Philippe possessed when intrigued.

Robert heaved a weary sigh. He pulled his gaze from Philippe and glanced up at the picture of his father hanging on the opposite wall. How odd that in this room he would utter almost the same announcement as his father had done so many years ago. The former duke had left him an estate, riches, title, and position. Regrettably, he also left Robert a legacy he did not expect—illness of a weakening heart. He learned from his physician that more than character traits passed from generation to generation.

The glass of brandy came to his lips, and he took a large gulp. He snickered as he looked at the cigar in this hand, remembering his father's nasty cough and jest over his smoking of the cigar in spite of his mounting health problems.

"My heart is ailing," Robert finally announced with little emotion. "Our physician has confirmed to me that I am in the early stages of heart failure." He finally lifted his eyes and looked at Philippe, who leaned forward in his seat. After digesting the shocking declaration, he spoke. His countenance bore sincere concern.

"Does Suzette know?"

"No, and I don't intend for her to know. Do you understand?" he firmly questioned.

"Perfectly," Philippe agreed. "She is a worrisome creature, and I doubt that she will be able to bear it."

"She suspects nothing now, but eventually as my conditions worsen, it will be impossible to keep hidden."

"Yes, of course. And what of Robert. Have you told him?"

"Not at this time. He has other things on his mind that are far more important than the slowly dying lump of flesh in my chest." Robert's eyes rose to his father's portrait. They peered back at him with the same stern gaze he had borne when alive. "*Stiff upper lip, boy*," he heard his voice clearly in his mind. Of course, he would bear his fate with dignity and concern for his family's well-being until they laid him in the grave next to his parents on the estate grounds.

"I find your news most distressing," Philippe admitted, breaking the awkward silence. His gaze fixated on the brandy in his glass as he slowly swirled it around before taking another sip. "Has the physician indicated anything about the progression?"

"You mean how long do I have to live? Just say it, Philippe. It is what it is." Robert echoed his father's words. "The physician cannot say for sure as it is a progressive illness. It could be a year or five for all I know."

Philippe appeared to have lost interest in his drink and cigar, snubbing out the flame and setting the glass down.

"It may sound like an empty cliché, but is there anything I can do for you?"

Philippe clutched his hands together and looked forlornly into Robert's eyes. His sincere voice gave Robert the strength he needed to continue.

"Yes, there is. It's the reason I pulled you aside." A lump formed in his throat betraying his anxiousness. Only a few feet away sat a man who nearly killed him for stealing his wife. He caused Philippe great harm and grief to win what he wanted. In retrospect, Robert admitted to himself that he ignored all conventions of good character and social behavior in his pursuit of Suzette. In the end, he nearly destroyed Philippe, taking from him family, livelihood, and his wife.

Nevertheless, admitting one's unscrupulous behavior did not necessarily mean that Robert bore any sorrow or regret regarding the outcome. He loved Suzette deeply, and their time together had been blissful, compared to his former marriage. Death did not frighten him, but facing what lay beyond the veil with her loving support at his side brought unbearable sadness. To compensate, he had to be sure before departing that she would be looked after.

"When I am gone, I want you to promise me that you will stay at Suzette's side and take care of her. She will not do well as a widow. We both are aware that once I am gone, old fears will return. Our son will be busy dealing with his new title, running the estate, and probably married by then with children of his own." He inhaled a deep breath in an attempt to calm the crackling of his voice. "I need reassurance she will not be alone, Philippe, so that I may rest in peace. Even if you must marry her to do so, I give you my blessing. However, I beg that you do not let her wither away the remainder of her life in inconsolable sadness."

After his words expelled, Robert anxiously awaited Philippe's response, who sat quietly thinking and staring at the carpet beneath his feet. Suddenly Philippe rose and stood in front of Robert, who followed suit. As they gazed at each other, Philippe reached out and placed his hand on Robert's shoulder.

"I am deeply grieved over your news. After all we have been through, I admit that I have nothing but great respect for you as a man." He paused and squeezed Robert's shoulder slightly. "I give you my word to watch over and care for Suzette's well-being as long as I am able to do so."

Exhaling a relieved sigh, a glimmer of contentment brightened his eyes. "Thank you." The anxious anticipation ended. No longer would he worry about Suzette or her welfare. Instead, he would focus upon living whatever days remained upon this earth without concern. Whether it be six months or a few years, he would live it to the fullest with his wife at his side.

"Well then, why don't we spend some time with your daughter and Suzette?" He wanted to say his wife, but there was no longer the need to reiterate his possession of the woman

Philippe once loved. It felt ironic to think that after all these years and what passed between them, he felt no hesitation in returning Suzette to his care. Whether she would accept any romantic notion on Philippe's behalf that ultimately resulted in remarriage, he would never know. Oddly enough, a part of Robert's heart wanted it to end that way even though he could not articulate the reason why. Perhaps making a full circle made sense.

CHAPTER 17

"Dessert?" the waiter inquired, removing their empty plates from the table.

"No dessert," Grace answered. "I'm afraid I have no room for another morsel to enter my stomach."

"That will be all," Robert agreed. "You can bring me the check."

"I feel ashamed," Grace said, silencing a small burp which she had no control of halting. "Why didn't you stop me from making a pig of myself, Robert?"

"There you go," Robert grinned. "Projecting your lack of control on me as if I forced the food down your throat."

"It makes me feel less guilty," Grace asserted. "Besides, you should take the blame for my appetite."

"Well, I haven't done anything that I know to increase your appetite unless you're eating for two, have I?" Robert grimaced at his playful insinuation.

"No, you've been a perfect gentleman." She winked. "For the most part."

"Now that's your fault," he laughed. "You've taken a perfectly respectable man and enticed him with your wiles."

"Oh, as if you hadn't been tempted and succumbed to temptation before I came along," Grace retorted in a low voice.

The waiter returned with the bill, and Grace watched as Robert opened his wallet. For some reason, even though it was a casual evening, he appeared more handsome than usual. Not that she ever thought him any less than handsome. It made her heart joyful knowing that they made a good couple. Their relationship felt like a perfect recipe of ingredients when mixed together created a sweet treat.

Robert appeared to have matured even during their courtship. Though at times he held a slight aristocratic air, Grace knew she balanced his personality. One day he would inherit his father's title. The responsibility would be great, but Robert's strong character, along with her support, would help him succeed. For the most part too, they enjoyed the same things in life. Their spats and disagreements were few, and laughter and teasing plentiful.

As far as physical attraction, Grace hungered for his touch every day. He possessed a way about him that made her knees weak, and kisses that sent shivers of pleasure down her body. On the other hand, her figure had a devastating effect on Robert. He made it quite apparent that her ample breasts were of great pleasure to him. When she watched him caress and kiss her, she could not understand why men adored a part of the female body meant for feeding babies. She giggled at the thought of his inability to keep his lips from her nipples.

When it came to other pleasures a man possessed under his clothes, a mystery remained. However, she was not as ignorant as most young women were her age who knew nothing about the intimacies of the marriage bed.

"What are you daydreaming about?" Robert asked. He looked at her quizzically.

"Nothing in particular." Of course she could not tell him where on his body her mind had wandered. Thinking of such things in a public setting made her wickedly depraved. It was his fault.

"It's a pleasant evening. Are you up for a something out of the ordinary?"

"Such as?"

Robert always came up with an impulsive idea to add a little excitement to their time together. "Come outside and let me show you." He offered his arm, and Grace took it.

As they exited the restaurant, she saw a fancy, open landau carriage. A driver stood by the two horses and tipped his hat as they drew near. It had been some time since Grace enjoyed a carriage ride. Motorcars were all the rage in London nowadays, creating outlandish traffic problems. Every mode of transportation clogged the highways from motorcars, hansom cabs, omnibuses, trollies, and old carriages.

"Is this for us?" she asked. She glanced at Robert, playing along with his surprise.

"Yes, my lady. I thought it would be a beautiful evening to take a carriage and drive down The Mall toward Buckingham Palace."

"What a splendid idea!" The sun had set, and gaslights illuminated the streets, creating a glowing pathway through the quieting city.

"Here, let me help you," Robert said, offering his hand.

She climbed into the carriage and sat down on the leather seat, and Robert joined her after speaking in a low tone to the driver.

"As you wish, sir," he acknowledged. With a short flick of the reins, the horses took their first steps, jolting them forward.

"It has been some time since I have walked St. James's Park toward the palace," Grace admitted with melancholy. "Life becomes so busy with frivolous things that even in London you often forget to enjoy your surroundings."

She leaned comfortably in the seat and felt Robert's arm wrap around her shoulder. The clip-clop of the horses' hooves on the cobblestone street echoed into the dimming scenery slowly giving way to darkness. A few stars brightened into visibility as the minutes passed.

"This is a wonderful surprise, Robert. Very relaxing," she said, snuggling closer.

"I'm curious to see the beginnings of the statue of Victoria," he said. "It's one of the reasons I wanted to take a moment in front of the palace."

"You're right, the Victoria Memorial," Grace responded. "Have they begun work already?"

"Yes, Sir Brock, from what I understand, has started the

sculpture. Unfortunately, it will be quite a few years before the unveiling, I'm afraid."

"I'm sure it will be a beautiful memorial to the Queen," Grace exclaimed. "I so admired her when growing up."

They neared Buckingham Palace, and the carriage slowed, coming to a stop. Construction had begun, but the monument had been fenced and draped to prevent the public from viewing.

"Well, I should have known," Robert said, sighing in disappointment. "Let's get out anyway," he suggested.

The driver opened the carriage door, and Robert helped her descend to the pavement below.

"Would you mind walking a bit in the park," Robert asked. "Let's find a bench by the lake and sit under the stars."

"Under the stars?" Grace shivered. "I'm afraid now that the sun has set, I'll be chilled," she complained like a spoiled child. Robert, of course, did the chivalrous act of removing his coat and draping it over her shoulders.

"Here, take this," he insisted.

"But will you be warm enough?"

"Don't worry about me."

Grace wrapped herself in the warmth. Her small frame disappeared underneath the fabric.

"All right, let's walk." She wrapped her arm around his and allowed him to lead her along the pathway into the park setting.

As their steps meandered down the pathway, flickers of light caught her attention. Not just one, but a row of illuminated candles circled a large oak tree. Off to the side, she recognized Robert's valet scurry away into the shadows. The sight caused a shiver to run down her spine.

"What are you up to, Robert Holland?"

Robert remained silent until they reached the location. Grace brought her hand to her mouth to silence a surprised gasp.

"Follow me," Robert whispered, gently pulling her into the flickering circle underneath the oak.

Grace knew by the look in Robert's eyes that the moment she dreamt about would soon transpire. Robert suddenly lowered himself onto one knee, reached inside his waistcoat pocket, and took out a ring. He grasped her hand and held it between his cold fingers.

"I brought you here, Grace Whitefield, to tell you that you have become the queen of my heart. There is no palace or monument to former queens that will ever match or surpass your beauty, charm, or amiable character."

As Grace listened to his confession, her heart pounded in her chest. She clutched his hand in return, trying her best to keep silent long enough for him to ask the question. He took a few seconds, cleared his throat, and then spoke. The flickering lights illuminated his eyes, and in them she beheld love.

"Will you marry me, Grace, and be the reigning woman of my life? I promise to adore, worship, and serve you," Robert paused and awkwardly continued. "That is if you'll have me."

If it were possible for a human heart to melt, Grace knew that her beating flesh would be lying at her feet in a puddle. Robert Holland, bended on one knee, had finally proposed. He held in his other hand a gorgeous ring, with an insanely large stone. A warm smile spread across her face as she recognized Robert's eyes turn anxious waiting for her response.

"Oh, Robert, yes, I'll marry you," she blurted.

Robert slipped the ring on her finger, rose to his feet, and swooped her up in his arms. He nearly knocked the breath from her lungs, pulling her into him and covering her mouth with a ravishing kiss that made her dizzy. Grace flung her arms around his neck and clung to him securely. It felt as if her soul passed into his body and took up residence. Something magical transpired between them, and she knew Robert felt it too.

"I've never felt anything like this," Robert gasped between breaths. "I've never fallen in love until you, Grace. You mean the world to me."

"I wish we could make love under the stars," Grace admitted. "Here, in the grass, surrounded by these candles."

"Oh, God, don't tempt me," Robert pleaded. "I could ravish every inch of you out in the open and feel no shame, but I'm afraid my valet may think unkindly of me."

"So you planned this, did you?"

"Yes, but I needed help to set up the candles and light them all," he chuckled.

"Kiss me anyway, Robert. Pull me down upon you in the grass and kiss me silly," Grace begged with a commanding dare.

Robert's wicked smile returned. "Dudley," Robert called out into the shadows.

"Yes, my lord?" the voice answered a few yards way.

"Take a walk and come back in a half hour. Everything is under control here."

"As you wish, my lord. Shall I have the driver bring the car around then as well?"

"I suppose," Robert answered. "Now go."

Grace giggled as she heard Dudley's footsteps meet the paved pathway and fade into the distance. The fleeting thought of someone seeing them in the dark crossed her mind, but she didn't care. After dropping to her knees, she pulled Robert down on top of her. A second later, his lips encircled her mouth. All of a sudden, Grace had a fleeting thought and pulled away.

"Did you ask my father if you could marry me?"

"Yes, and your brother," Robert assured, clamping his lips over her mouth.

Apparently, permission had been granted, and Grace enjoyed the passion of Robert's kisses enshrined in the joy of their lives ahead.

—·✳·—

When Robert returned to the Holland estate, he felt as if he were walking on clouds. After all the agonizing and procrastination, he had taken the step and proposed. In a few months he would be a married man.

"In a few months!"

He echoed his thoughts aloud and recognized that Grace successfully talked him into setting a date on their short ride back to her home. The way that he felt, he would have given her anything she wanted. The last hour was turning into a fog of what he agreed or did not agree to about their wedding. Grace skillfully wound him around her little finger.

Upon his arrival, he thought everyone would have retired since the hour was late. To his surprise, he discovered his mother and Philippe alone in the parlor having a drink together. The scene caused him to hesitate in the doorway. It only took a moment before his mother saw his arrival.

"Am I interrupting anything," he said, walking in and standing before them. He glanced around the room and wondered why his father left the two of them alone. "Where is Father?"

"Asleep, I'm afraid," Suzette said. "He retired early complaining of being tired."

"And Jolene?"

"In her room," Philippe answered. "Contemplating her solitary existence, I would think."

"How did it go?" his mother inquired with anticipation in her voice.

"Very well, actually." Robert smirked. He felt like blurting out the news but held his tongue. He nonchalantly wandered over to a nearby chair and sat down. No doubt his actions were irritating his mother, but he enjoyed the tease.

"Did she say yes?"

"Yes to what?" Philippe quipped.

"Grace will marry me," Robert proudly announced. A broad grin spread across his face.

"Oh, my goodness," Suzette yelped. "You are engaged!"

"Good for you," Philippe said, rising to his feet. He enthusiastically shook Robert's hand. "Congratulations. Splendid young lady."

"Indeed, she is a grand young lady," Robert repeated.

"Have you set a date?" His mother's eyes beamed with anticipation.

"October," Robert replied.

"So soon?" Suzette raised her brow.

"Any particular reason for the rush?" Philippe said with a straight face.

In light of their comments and raised brow, Robert concluded they were wondering if there had been another reason for the rush to the altar.

"There is nothing untoward," Robert said, conveying the answer without saying the obvious. "We both agreed to forgo an extended engagement."

"It's a bit out of the ordinary," his mother noted. "I pity Grace's family, as they will be running around in a frantic trying to prepare on such short notice."

Robert laughed. "I have a sneaking suspicion that Grace has already decided upon her dress and trousseau, so it may not be as overwhelming as you contemplate."

"Needless to say, Robert, I am extremely pleased and happy for you," his mother repeated.

"Well, I'm exhausted. If you will be so kind as to excuse me," Robert said, rising to his feet, "I'm going to retire."

As they bid him good night, he could not believe that his mother and Philippe sat together so amicably having an evening drink. Old wounds apparently healed where Robert thought scars remained. Even his father seemed to have enjoyed Philippe's presence during his visit with Jolene. Odd as the picture appeared, Robert had other things to ponder. While Grace would be primping and powdering her nose, he had a honeymoon to plan.

CHAPTER 17

Jolene knew that her attitude bordered on the ridiculous. The evening before at supper, she felt dreadful. All she could think about was James and why he departed in such haste. Naturally, she blamed Robert for frightening him away with his scowls and veiled threats. On the other hand, she needed to give James the benefit of the doubt. He had a way of quickly stripping her of any dignity she possessed as a woman of title. Her mind could not even remember her status in life when he was nearby. The best course of action would be to blame him completely for her current predicament.

After everyone awakened and joined for breakfast, she determined to reign in her foul mood lest they think she was an immature child. When she gathered her portion from the side table and sat down, her mother spoke.

"I believe that Robert has an announcement to make."

Jolene glanced around the table. Her mother and father were grinning from ear to ear, and the duke had a knowing smile on his face.

"What announcement?" Jolene wondered, turning to Robert.

"I asked Grace Whitefield to marry me, and she has graciously accepted my proposal. The ceremony will be held at St. Martin-in-the-Fields on October 22 of this year."

Robert radiated such joy over the announcement that it left Jolene in a state of utter shock. Of course a part of her hoped or even anticipated that one day he would fall in love with Grace. Nevertheless, as the realization of what would soon transpire, Jolene experienced a terrible gnawing in the pit of her stomach. Naturally, she should have felt overwhelming joy at the announcement but instead felt the prick of jealousy. It was not until she realized that everyone at the table waited for her to say something.

"Well done," her father exclaimed, giving Jolene a prodding glance to join in the celebration.

Ashamed that she entertained such terribly selfish emotions, she flashed a huge smile albeit a painful one.

"Oh, Robert, how wonderful! Grace's dream of winning your heart has been granted. I'm so happy for the two of you."

Jolene remembered the day when Grace first professed her affections. After so many years of barely noticing the young lady, she somehow won his heart. *How very clever of her*, Jolene thought.

"Don't forget you had your hand in it," Robert said. "You slyly encouraged me for some time to take notice of her affections."

"And I encouraged her to be patient, which apparently aided as well," she said.

"Excuse me," the butler announced, entering the dining room. "But there is a delivery for the komtesse." In his hands he held a bouquet of red roses.

Upon seeing the blooms, all painful enviousness vanished. Jolene's heart burst with joy. James had not forgotten her after all.

"Well, I wonder who those could be from," Robert said, pulling his mouth to one side.

"They are beautiful," Jolene gushed. She took the bouquet in her arms, searching for a card.

"One of her admirers," Philippe murmured.

A worrying thought flitted through her mind, hoping it wasn't Alastair attempting to win her affections due to Robert's announcement. With her hands shaking, she pulled the card out and read the handwritten note aloud. "*Begging your forgiveness for my quick departure. Yours, James.*"

"For a moment there, I thought Alastair might be welcoming you as his future sister-in-law," Robert chortled.

"Well, it seems as if the mysterious gentleman is alive and well," her father said.

The snide remarks confirmed to Jolene that neither Robert nor her father felt any endearment toward James.

"Then I shall send the invitation to the dinner party posthaste," her mother remarked.

"What dinner party?" Robert's head swung agitatedly in her direction.

"You know," his father grimaced. "A dinner party, filled with an extravagant menu, guests filling our home, and your mother stretching my budget to capacity."

"You needn't go to such extremes," Jolene said.

"Nonsense." Her mother scowled playfully at Robert. "My husband is merely playing a stern role to tease me to no end."

"And it's my pleasure to do so," he endearingly added.

"I insist that we use this opportunity as well," Suzette added, "to celebrate Robert's engagement. Grace's family must come too and partake of the festivities."

"And what of my sister, Marguerite, and her husband?" Robert cautiously probed.

"Oh, I hadn't thought of that matter," Suzette admitted. "Would it be considered extremely rude not to invite Geoffrey?"

"Don't you dare ask Geoffrey," Robert balked at his mother. "You will be guilty of setting up a firestorm. With Alastair and I together in the same room, along with this strange James fellow, it will turn into a bloody disaster."

The room filled with tension as Robert resolutely made his sentiments known. Jolene silently panicked at the thought of them all meeting at one time. It would make for a ruinous affair.

"I will speak privately with Marguerite," the duke announced. "She will understand our choice for excluding Geoffrey. Should they be offended, they may forgo the dinner party altogether."

As Jolene clutched the beautiful flowers in her arms, her emotions were torn. Everyone spoke with joyous remarks for Robert's good fortune. On the other hand, only her mother appeared to care at all about her feeling for James. The duke, Robert, and her father gave no positive comment as if they dreaded the ensuing affair. Why couldn't they support her desire to find a husband?

Jolene rose to her feet. "If you will excuse me, I'm going to find the housekeeper to put these in a vase and bring them to my room." She glanced at Robert's disgruntled expression. "I am so very happy for the two of you, dearest."

Robert nodded. "Thank you."

As she left the dining room, she hoped that James would accept her mother's invitation to dine at the Holland estate. It would not be the ideal situation in which to spend time with him, surrounded by her suspicious family members. Nevertheless, it would afford her another opportunity to enjoy his charismatic personality.

With her mind filled with thoughts of James, she halted her steps when a hand grabbed her shoulder. Surprised at the accosting halt, she spun around to see her father a mere foot away. Instantly, by the narrowness of his gaze, she knew an unpleasant conversation would ensue.

"Do you realize that your attitude is alienating your family?"

"What attitude?" Jolene protested with a huff.

"Your strained congratulatory remarks to Robert were evident to everyone at the table. Are these flowers that important that you cannot remain to celebrate his engagement?" His hand reached for the bouquet, but Jolene stepped back and pulled it from his grasp.

"Of course I'm happy for Robert. I merely wished to put these into a vase."

Philippe studied her, but Jolene could sense that he was not convinced of her remark. She retreated into her thoughts and lowered her gaze to the flowers in her arms. The bright red roses were brilliant in color and vibrant, giving her hope for the possibilities that might await her future.

"Hopefully, someday I will find love too and will announce my good news," she sighed.

"You seem convinced already that this good news revolves around this young man that has obviously captured your heart,"

Philippe said. "I look forward to meeting him, frankly."

"It worries me that this dinner party will turn into an unfavorable examination by you and the other guests. All I want is time to get to know him better," she pleaded. "Do be kind to him. I don't wish to die of embarrassment."

Philippe smirked at her request. "I shall keep an open mind."

"Good," Jolene replied. "Now, if you'll excuse me, my flowers need water." She turned from her father and proceeded down the hall. With a worried frown, she clung tightly to the bouquet, praying to heaven that the dinner party would not turn into a disastrous affair.

--·✳·--

James Derrington discovered the delights of London early in his arrival. He only visited the bustling city a few times with his family as a child. Now, as an adult, walking the streets and partaking of the cultural activities were more exciting than the gray skies of the north.

As he sat sipping an ale at a discreet pub not far from his hotel, he pondered his current state of affairs. Even though he had bragged about coming from an influential family in York, he had never stepped foot in the city filled with its medieval architecture and impressive abbey. Instead, he had been born in Liverpool. A speech tutor to match the tone of the upper class had refined his lazy northern drawl. To add to his education, he extensively studied the history of York, its surrounding countryside, and the Derrington lineage, lest questions were directed to him in conversation.

The past month of refinement turned him into a dashing young man of status and class. He rather liked the recrafting of his identity. Leaving behind his dull life and donning a hat, cane, and expensive clothing with shiny shoes had been delightful. In spite of his current role as Viscount James Derrington, he was determined to bury the simple name that had been given at birth. He had been hired by his benefactor to play an elaborate ploy on Komtesse von Lamberg.

After finishing his drink, he returned to the Savoy and its

extravagant environment. His sponsor insisted that the hotel be his residence while in London. He gladly agreed to the high-scale lodgings with a large suite of rooms to accommodate his stay. With a new wardrobe and a wallet full of crisp pound notes, he easily slipped into the role of a viscount in London on business. Perhaps he should feel guilty, but in actuality, his visit was purely business of sorts. He arrived to carry out a professional arrangement.

He reached the front desk to check for messages, anticipating one from Jolene. The fresh bouquet of red roses was for the purpose of obtaining her absolution for his quick departure the night before. In retrospect, he should not have turned down the invitation to dine with Lord Holland and his lovely young lady. Jolene appeared mortified when he gave his insincere apology. Out of the blue, his rare conscience raised its ugly head for playing with the affections of the young woman.

Even though she was clearly out of his league, he found her company to be pleasant and her dark beauty alluring. As he stood there listening to her half brother suggest dinner, he wanted to flee the ruse. As his remorse began turning his palms cold, he knew that he needed a moment of privacy to reign in his emotions and solidify his intent to keep faithful to the task at hand. Naturally, his mission carried the risk of emotional involvement. He could not allow that to happen under any circumstances.

"Are there any messages for me?" He peeked over the side of the counter.

"Viscount Derrington," the clerk responded, immediately recognizing him. "As a matter of fact, this arrived within the last half hour." He held out an ivory parchment envelope.

"Thank you." James snatched it from the clerk's hand. With an initial glance at the note, he became aware that it arrived from the Holland estate. The lobby was no place to read its contents, so James slipped it into his inner vest pocket.

"Thank you," he said, nodding congenially to the clerk.

When he arrived back at his suite of rooms, he sat down leisurely on a chair by the window overlooking The Strand. He broke the seal and pulled out a piece of paper. To his surprise, it had not been penned by Jolene but by the hand of the duchess.

His eyes brightened and a smirk curled the corner of his lips as he read the invitation to dine at the Holland estate.

"Oh, bravo," he shouted. "I've apparently been forgiven."

James folded the note and replaced it in his inside pocket. Soon he would be in the presence of Jolene and no doubt carefully examined by a household of family members. The invitation afforded him more time with her and provided an additional inroad to her weak will. The course appeared clear of obstructions. He would win her heart, delight in sexual spoils, and abandon her to social ruination. Nevertheless, he needed to curtail his damnable ounce of a conscience so as not to spoil his goal. For two hundred pounds, he would gladly suppress any sense of right and wrong. When the ruse finally ended, he would have enough money and a free ticket to leave behind his dreary life of servitude and move to the Americas.

CHAPTER 18

"Viscount Derrington," the butler bellowed as he stood on the threshold of the Holland's grand parlor. James surveyed the room, and a lump formed in his throat. The affair was not a private dinner party but a large gathering of family and friends. He sucked in a deep breath and took a few steps toward Jolene, who swiftly came to his rescue. Undoubtedly, she recognized the panic in his eyes.

"I am so pleased to see you," she greeted him with a broad grin. Her heady perfume of sweet musk wafted up his nose, which drew his eyes downward to her ample bosom plumped in her bodice. Realizing that he gave away his adoration far too soon by the sparkle in his eyes, Jolene wrapped her arm around his and led him into the den of scrutiny.

"May I introduce you to His Grace and my mother, the Duchess."

Jolene's voice trembled, which incited him to dispel his uneasiness. The time to pour on the charm had arrived. He bowed his head in deference.

"It is indeed a pleasure to meet you."

"The pleasure is all mine," the duke replied.

"And am I to assume that the invitation to dine with you this evening was written in your lovely penmanship?" He smiled at the duchess, who studied him with interest. Even though she appeared middle-aged, her striking features were unparalleled.

"My daughter has spoken favorably of you, and we thought it only natural to invite you to dine with us this evening."

Taken aback by her French accent, he immediately found her an agreeable soul. Nevertheless, the remainder of attendees appeared to stare at him suspiciously. Jolene's half brother and Grace stood to the left.

"Lord Holland, it is a pleasure to see you again," he said, offering his hand in a polite handshake. Surprisingly, Robert took it with no hesitation.

"Miss Whitefield, you are beaming," he said, noting the undeniable radiance of her face. A nearby gentleman, whose speech betrayed his French origins, provided the reason.

"We are also celebrating the engagement of Robert and lovely Grace this evening," he added.

"Viscount, may I introduce you to my father, Philippe Moreau," Jolene clarified.

James rapidly counted the relationships that were decidedly rather strange. Her mother married the duke, but her father was seemingly welcomed as anyone else. The situation surely must have had some scandalous history to discover. Unfortunately, he had not been given the full picture from his benefactor beforehand.

Another man stepped forward and offered his hand. James immediately recognized him from the masquerade as Jolene's escort.

"Mr. Whitefield, am I correct? You are Grace's brother."

"Alastair Whitefield," he responded. "I'm impressed that you remembered my name."

The unwelcome glare in the man's eyes conveyed his dislike. James had taken away the affections of Jolene from this gentleman, which explained the dark look of jealousy in his eyes. Definitely sensing his loathing hatred, James decided to interact little with the sullen chap.

The atmosphere in the room felt decidedly unfriendly, but James stood firm and confident before his judges. Everyone's eyes held a glint of distrust toward him, except for Jolene and her mother.

"We were sorry to see you disappear so speedily after the

opera," her half brother suddenly remarked.

"Yes, it was dreadfully inconsiderate of me. It appears my absolution wrapped in a dozen red roses has gained me clemency though."

"Apparently," Robert drawled sarcastically.

"Well, I must add congratulatory remarks to you, Lord Holland, and your lovely young lady," James offered.

"We all hoped that the relationship would blossom into a wedding," Jolene said. "Grace is the dearest, you see, and I think that I had my hand in a bit of matchmaking with the two of them."

"As Grace's brother and Robert's best friend, I had my own say in the matter as well," Alastair added.

"Indeed and laced with the threats of a broken nose should I misbehave in my pursuit," Robert quipped with a jovial smirk.

"Are you here in London for very long?"

James turned toward Jolene's father, whose voice sounded friendlier.

"That depends, sir, on how long it takes me to complete my business. I imagine another three to four weeks."

"And then will you return to York?" the duke asked.

"Perhaps," James replied. "I may continue on holiday for a bit longer before returning to my responsibilities at home."

Luckily, the sound of the gong saved him from further interrogation.

"Dinner is served," the butler announced in the parlor doorway.

James offered his arm to Jolene, who glanced at him adoringly. Each time he lowered his eyes to her short stature, her cleavage met his gaze. If nothing else, his task of seduction would be an enjoyable event.

As they walked into the large dining hall, James found himself engulfed in a lavish room. For most of his life, he had dined at a wooden table no bigger than a few feet in length and breadth. A huge cherry-wood dining table adorned with sparkling crystal glasses and fine bone china centered the room. Two footmen stood at attention ready to serve.

He noted the place cards on the table and found himself seated, thankfully, next to Jolene. His mind whirled in circles as he recanted in his thoughts which of the numerous pieces of cutlery and glasses were to be used for dinner. Hopefully, he would be able to keep up the façade as he kept at bay any disgusting habits he previously had been accustomed to elsewhere.

Dinner ensued, and James settled into a leisurely discussion maintaining his own amongst the room of aristocrats who sat across the table. Jolene's father exhibited no airs of status, though the duke and his lovely wife, as well as Robert, were tainted with the usual upper-class mentalities. On the other hand, Alastair Whitefield's continual scowling scrutiny throughout the dinner hour became increasingly unwelcome. At times he felt like balling his fist and punching him in the jaw, which he deemed far too square to make the man handsome enough for Jolene.

At a dull moment when others fell into conversation with someone other than the two of them, Jolene leaned into him and whispered.

"I so wish that we might find time alone." She heaved a heavy sigh, glancing about the table hoping that her indiscretion had not been noted.

"Yes, the situation makes it difficult to get to know one another." James knew that the evening would not afford any privacy after dinner either. The days ahead would undoubtedly present the same challenge. Then unexpectedly he decided to move things favorably in his direction.

"Hampton Court," he blurted out. Conversations ceased and heads turned in his direction. "You know, I've never traveled down the Thames to see the infamous structure that once housed Henry VIII. Is it as grand as they say?"

The duke's left eyebrow rose surprised over the inquiry. "I'm surprised you've never been."

James shrugged his shoulders. "I'm quite sure my parents have toured the grounds and buildings, but I've never been afforded the opportunity."

"Well, why don't we visit together," Jolene suggested. "I have not seen it either."

An awkward silence followed amidst concerned frowns.

"Well, I would like to see the palace," Philippe stated. "If you don't mind me accompanying the two of you, we can make it a threesome."

There had been no doubt in James's mind that he would not be allowed to take Jolene without an escort. Her father appeared eager enough. Perhaps they would be able to slip away so he could steal a kiss but that wasn't the point. He needed to get her totally alone. Otherwise, his quest to seduce her would never come around.

"I do wish that you would give me the opportunity to spend a moment with him unaccompanied," Jolene protested, glancing at her father. "Would it be so terrible if we spent the day together in public?"

James's head spun in Jolene's direction astonished over her brash complaint. The young lady had spunk, and he liked it. As much as he hated to disagree, he knew that unless he acted sensibly over the matter, they'd think him brash as well. Carefully he tempered his counter so as not to dissuade any possibility of success.

"I understand your family's concern completely," he began. He felt a surprising quiver in his vocal cords and cleared his throat before continuing. "I am a stranger here." James scanned the dinner guests, noting Alastair's disapproving and dagger-like stare.

"Well, I see no problem with it," the duchess countered with a grin. "Jolene is a grown woman. It's about time we put aside these outdated formalities."

"Mother." Robert's lips tightened in a straight line showing his displeasure.

"Well, your mother has a point," the duke interjected. "They will be in a public setting, and I think we owe it to Jolene to trust her own good senses." He looked at Jolene's father. "Philippe, what say you? Would you mind visiting Hampton Court in the coming weeks? Suzette and I would be happy to take you on an outing."

James's eyes darted back and forth, waiting for Jolene's father to reply.

Rather than quickly agreeing, he pulled his mouth to one side and fiddled with the knife at the side of his plate. The choice of cutlery while pondering his decision inferred a hidden message in his hesitation. "I have my reservations but agree," Philippe spouted with agitation.

James glanced over at Jolene's half brother, scowling back in his direction.

"Thank you for the confidence you have shown to us both," he said. "I assure you that I shall treat her with the greatest respect."

"I know you will," Jolene answered.

Her confident gaze sent another shiver of guilt coursing down his spine. Of course, his intentions were completely without honor. If he had his way with her, there would not be an ounce of respect to offer.

Dinner resumed at a leisurely pace with superficial chitchat. As usual, James assumed that afterward the men would retreat for brandy and cigars while the women went for tea together in the parlor. However, to his surprise, Jolene's action saved him from the ordeal.

"I'm taking James into the gardens for a walk," she announced. Everyone conceded rather than arguing the point. Without making further apologies to anyone, she took him by the arm and led him outdoors for an evening stroll.

"Finally," she heaved in relief. "I'm so sorry for the unbearable scrutiny you have received, especially from Robert and Alastair."

James chuckled. Their male domination over his presence had been quite humorous, actually. "Think nothing of it," he grinned. "They do so because they care." He hesitated and decided to pursue a singular point. "It appears that Mr. Whitefield harbors affectionate feelings for you. Am I correct in my assumption?"

Jolene gave his arm a tug, bringing him close to her side as they strolled. "Yes, he's in love with me, but I do not reciprocate his adoration."

"Might I ask why?"

Suddenly Jolene stopped and turned toward him. An undeniable glint of affection filled her eyes, and a softness in her voice answered his question.

"Because you have stolen my heart," she confessed. "I am helpless when we are together." She lowered her head apparently embarrassed over her admission.

The tips of James's fingers lifted her chin until he caught her gaze and captured her thoughts with his own. "I will admit that I have planned all along to steal your heart, my dearest. If anyone is helpless in your presence, it is I."

Jolene closed her eyes, and James instinctively grasped the moment to kiss her moist lips. He drew her into his body and encircled his arms around her tiny frame, making it impossible for her to protest. She fell limp into his embrace as his mouth searched out hers with his tongue. An overwhelming urge to fondle her breasts brought a swift erection that she instantly felt pressed against her frame. A second later, she pulled away. He released her, and she stepped back, her face filled with alarm.

"I will not apologize," he spoke out of breath. "My desire for you is undeniable."

The flush in her cheeks spoke of her own heated physical response.

"James," she whispered.

"Don't be afraid of me," he said, drawing close to her once again. "You are a beautiful and intelligent woman who has touched my heart deeply. I do admire you." He brought his hand to the side of her warm cheek and caressed it in his palm. A slow, relieved smile replaced the anxiety.

"Perhaps we should return indoors," she said. "I think it would be safer."

A chuckle rattled his throat. "Yes, perhaps it would be wise." He offered her his arm, trying to suppress the sly grin over his impending conquest. He only required a private room and locked door to complete his directive. Obviously, with a bit more affectionate wooing on his part, Jolene would be an easy conquest to gain his waiting pay.

As they approached the veranda, James caught the glares of Robert and Alastair watching them through the window. He could not help but return his own rueful disdain with a narrowed gaze. The two were unquestionably getting on his nerves.

-·✻·-

"I can tell he is annoyed that he's seen us watching," Robert said. "Good." He swung around and headed for the decanter of brandy.

"Obviously, you don't like the man," his father interjected while puffing on his cigar.

"Neither of us does," Alastair confirmed. He held out his glass to Robert to fill his as well.

"Frankly, I'm not sure what to think about him," Philippe added. "I mean what is the worry about, anyway? He will go back to York and Jolene to Vienna. Nothing will come of it."

"Let us hope," Robert said, sitting down in an empty chair.

"We should know more in a few days," Alastair announced. He took a sip and grinned.

His father did not let the statement go unobserved. "Explain."

"We both hired a private detective to investigate his affairs," Robert announced. "Of course, I could have saved a few quid if Alastair would have told me he had engaged someone before I paid my invoice." He smirked mischievously.

"You must be kidding," Philippe balked, leaning forward in his chair. "Does Jolene know?"

"Oh, good God, no," Robert exclaimed. "I'm not that daft to let her know. She would never forgive me." He glanced at Alastair. "Besides, he can justify his actions because he's in love with her."

His father and Philippe simultaneously swung their heads in Alastair's direction. It appeared comical.

"Is that right?" Philippe said with a beaming smile.

"Regardless of my affections," Alastair dismissed, "Robert and I suspect there is something troublesome about the viscount. It's a matter of Jolene's safety."

"Well, perhaps it is for her own good," his father agreed.

"I'll admit," Philippe said, "it does provide me with some comfort over the matter that the two of you have taken it upon yourselves to dig into his background. Do let us know what becomes of it."

"Definitely," Alastair assured. "I'll be the first to expose the man."

A knock came at the door, which afterward opened revealing Suzette, Grace, Jolene, and the viscount. The men rose to their feet to greet their arrival.

"Are we interrupting anything?" Suzette walked over to the duke as if she knew the answer.

"Just brandy and cigars," Robert replied. "Would you like a glass, Viscount?"

"Yes, that sounds enjoyable." He walked passed Alastair ignoring him.

Robert handed over the brandy. "Enjoy," he said. He wondered how long they would have to wait for an answer from the private detectives.

CHAPTER 19

Jolene agreed upon the duke's insistence that they allow his driver to take them to Hampton Court, fully aware that they probably would tip him extra for watching over their whereabouts. James did not seem to mind the least, and their arrival at the palace afforded them the opportunity to be alone.

As they strolled through the buildings where Henry VIII and his many wives had lived, Jolene felt a shudder down her spine.

"I don't understand how he could chop off their heads. What a despicable man," she moaned, walking the hall where Catherine Howard begged for her life. James merely chuckled. "You don't think it is terrible that he had her beheaded?" Jolene scowled at his cold reaction.

James stopped. "She's the resident ghost," he whispered. "Shall we wait here and see if she appears?"

"Oh, stop it," Jolene said, pulling him along. "I wanted this day to be filled with excitement, not morbid fear."

After hastening her step down the hall with James in tow, she glanced around until other visitors had passed. It did not take long for him to take advantage of the opportunity by lowering his lips to hers and giving her a stolen kiss. Jolene loved the warmth of his mouth and the tingling sensation experienced during their tender moments. When they heard voices approach, they quickly parted, both smiling impishly at one another.

"We are still not alone," James complained, heaving a sigh.

"Must we return with the duke's driver? We can easily take a cab and spirit ourselves away for a few more hours of privacy." A couple passed by, making his point.

"You are quite right. We are together in public but not really alone." Jolene waited until the couple passed. "I can tell the driver we will take another transportation home," she said, turning to do so.

"No," James swiftly responded, grabbing her upper arm to stop her step. "Let's make a game of it. We can hail a cab and return in a few hours. Let's go for a spot of tea somewhere and a light lunch."

"Well, I suppose that wouldn't harm anything," she agreed. "He'll never know what we've done if we do return with him later."

James pulled out a brochure and pointed to an escape route. "I think if we follow this corridor, it will lead us to an exit. It's far from his view."

"That leads to the Lion Gate," Jolene commented. "Look, there is an inn just down the road. Perhaps we can order tea and lunch there." Jolene brought her hand to her mouth and laughed. "Oh, dear, from one public setting to another. I dare say, we shall be in the same predicament."

"True," James said, stroking his chin. "We could rent a private room and order room service," he suggested. "Should anyone find out, I'm afraid it would create quite a scandal with your family."

"I won't tell them if you won't," Jolene jested, taking his hand and pulling him down the corridor.

"My lips are sealed." A broad grin spread across his face.

Without being seen by the driver, they swiftly departed and exited through the Lion Gate onto Hampton Road. The inn, only a few yards away from the entrance, appeared quaint enough. Jolene surmised that no one would be the wiser as to their identities. However, for the sake of discreetness, James inquired at the desk without Jolene at his side for a room. After being able to procure a lodging, he headed up the stairs. Jolene, acting like another guest, nonchalantly followed behind at a leisurely gait. It felt like a playful ploy rather than a scandalous rendezvous.

Unnoticed by anyone, James slipped the key into the room, Jolene ran through the doorway, and he swiftly shut it. The two of them burst into laughter at the absurdity of their little game. When the hilarious moment had passed, James's smile faded. Replaced with an intense gaze of desire, it brought a shiver of cold reality that she had just entered a bedchamber with a man she barely knew. What had she been thinking?

"Can you ring for room service?" Her voice quavered slightly, betraying her nerves. "I am famished."

"Let me check if there is a menu." James walked over to a side table and examined the contents. "Ah, here is one," he said, snatching it in his hand and giving it to Jolene. "Order whatever you wish, my love."

His words of endearment swept the corner of her lips upward. "What sounds good," she mused. Her eyes glazed over the content, but nothing registered. Concentration proved impossible. "A watercress sandwich and tea sounds delightful enough for me. What would you like?"

James hesitated, looking at the menu she held in her hand. His eyes lifted until he caught Jolene with intensity and desire.

"You," he whispered.

He stepped forward and took her in his arms, placing his warm lips over her mouth. She swooned over his invasive tongue and dropped the menu to the floor. The proficiency of his kissing had been unlike anything she experienced before. Her body ached for satisfaction.

Afterward, James placed his arms underneath her and carried her to the bed putting her down upon the soft coverlet. Jolene, paralyzed by anticipation, made no objection. The craving in his eyes and the throbbing hunger she felt in her body enhanced her recklessness. Whatever thoughts she once possessed of propriety vanished.

As James hovered above her, he searched her eyes for her willingness to go beyond a romantic kiss. She gulped, thinking of the consequences that could ensue if she gave in to his enticement. Suddenly he removed his coat and unbuttoned his shirt. Her eyes widened at the sight of his bare chest and muscular arms. He tossed aside the white linen, standing before her in all his glory. Would she be next to bare everything?

"I adore you," he said in a sultry voice. "In fact, I love you." He approached and laid alongside her body, tenderly stroking her hair.

Hearing his confession brought a smile to her face. "Oh, James, I love you too."

Unexpectedly his hand cupped her breast. Before she could vocalize an objection, his tongue pushed between her lips deep into her mouth. Jolene moaned over the assault entering her body. Each movement made her weaker underneath his massive frame. For a second he pulled away, and she gasped for breath.

"Let me make love to you," he pleaded, playing with her nipple, squeezing it just enough to drive her mad. "I do so wish to make you my wife."

Electricity shot through her body, arousing her sexuality. The first taste of passion tempted her severely, and she teetered on the brink of losing control.

"We shouldn't." She halfheartedly protested. Even though the moral implications brought guilt, she wanted to experience the unknown. Would it be so wrong? They loved each other. He spoke of marriage.

"I want to be one with you. Let me teach you pleasure, my love."

As she lay underneath him desperately wanting to know what it would be like, her hesitation caused something in his eyes to change. His desire turned to desperation. The spoken words of love were betrayed by actions. One hand continued to squeeze her breast harder while the other had craftily found its way between her legs inching slowly upward. James pulled at her bodice nearly ripping the seam as he clawed at her to relent to his advances. Rather than tenderly enticing her to make love, she had somehow become his prey to devour. A weak protest escaped her lips.

"Stop, James, please," she pleaded, squirming beneath him. He continued his aggressive movements, ignoring her plea.

Reminiscent of the terrible event with Geoffrey, her uncontrollable desire instantaneously turned to panic. Her heart raced in her chest. No longer did she see James but rather the unsavory and sickening face of Geoffrey flashed before her eyes. The thought revolted her to such an extent that Jolene recoiled in disgust and brutally slapped James across the face.

"Stop!"

Her shrieking voice and assault made its point, and James froze his actions. At first she thought he would retaliate in anger as she cowered, anticipating a return blow. Instead, he slowly rose to his feet and hovered over her trembling body. A mournful expression furrowed his brow at her disheveled state.

"He said you would be easy," he blubbered. His breathing, heavy and labored, exposed his frustration. "Bloody hell, Jolene! You won't let me go through with this, will you?" Agitated, James raked his hands through his hair and turned away from her sight.

Shocked at his words, Jolene shot up in bed and bellowed. "Who? Who said I would be easy?"

He shook his head as if to say he would not answer. Instead, he continued to grumble with his back turned away.

"If you won't give it to me, I'm not about to rape you to get my due." He flopped on a chair and held his hands in his head. "I really like you, but it's not worth it," he groaned.

Astonished at his confession, Jolene rose to her feet. Her body shuddered, trying to make sense of his babbling.

"James Derrington, if you don't clarify for me this entire situation, I'm going to slap you again and enjoy it immensely."

Gradually he lifted his head. "I deserved the last one," he admitted, rubbing the side of his face marked with her stinging smack. "I might as well spit it out and be done with it."

"Then spit, for heaven's sake," she hissed.

"You'll hate me for it," he remarked. A sad expression wrinkled his handsome face. He opened his mouth as if to speak and then shut it again.

"Tell me!"

After a few moments of dolefully gazing at her as she hovered above him, he confessed.

"Geoffrey Chambers paid me to seduce you. He wanted me to win your affections, play the attentive, loving male, and take your virginity."

Stunned, Jolene's mouth gaped open. Seconds slipped by as she attempted to process the revelation.

"Afterward, I had been instructed to slip a sleeping potion in your tea, so you would spend the night here and awaken to find me gone."

"I don't understand," she cried in anger. "At the ball, you came to my rescue."

"Planned, I'm afraid." James shrugged his shoulders in indifference. "Geoffrey anticipated that you would find me more debonair than Alastair after my daring rescue. He was right about that much."

When she recalled the moment and how she had fallen for James's savior-like actions and handsome appearance, something inside her soul snapped. Whether her heart broke in half or her anger exploded the tissue in her chest, Jolene could not discern. She burst forth screaming her words.

"How much, damn it?" she heaved. "How much did he pay you for this scam?"

Instinctively, James drew back in the chair obviously concerned that she would physically wallop him once more.

"Two hundred pounds and a ticket on The White Star ship line to New York."

A flurry of German curses spewed from Jolene's dry mouth. After expelling her anger, she swallowed the lump in her throat that choked her intake of air. As her chest rose rapidly up and down, she thought she would faint. When he saw her physical distress, James jumped to his feet, taking a step toward her. He reached out to steady her stance, but she jerked backward out of his grasp.

"I can't do it, Jolene," he cried. "Not to say that I'm not a blackguard myself and bloody devious, but if forcing you is what I have to do to get paid, it's not worth it."

She stared at him, wondering who had swept her off her feet in a matter of weeks. It pained her to ask, but she had to know.

"Who are you?" Her eyes narrowed at him in distrust. "Is there really a Viscount James Derrington somewhere in England?"

"My name is Henry Mead," he answered. "I'm from

Liverpool."

Henry Mead, she repeated in her mind. The shocking reality of his common name and lack of title stripped him of everything she once admired. An extreme heaviness crushed her chest as she gazed at the man who stood before her acting like a scolded schoolboy. The once charismatic male, who she had fallen desperately in love within a matter of weeks, had vanished before her eyes.

After all of Robert's and Alastair's warnings, they had been right. She had been duped by Geoffrey and nearly ruined. It frightened her to think how close she had come to allowing him to have his way with her and how much she ached for it! What a dreadful outcome it would have been had she succumbed. She could have become pregnant out of wedlock. Thankfully, an ounce of goodness had kept him from forcing himself upon her without permission. She owed him that much.

Then, at that heartbreaking instant, it became apparent. She could not let Geoffrey win.

"I will pay you double the money to tell that bastard you completed the deed."

"What?" He tilted his head, gaping at her in astonishment.

"You heard me. Another two hundred pounds in your pocket."

"Oh, I couldn't take your money," he said, shaking his head and turning away.

"Call it the price of passion," Jolene sarcastically retorted. She reached out and grabbed his arm, pulling him to a standstill. "You nearly ruined me because I fell in love with you. Don't you think you owe me at least that much to help me get back at that bastard?" Tears stung her eyes. "If you do as I say, I'll give you the money, and you can leave England." Her voice, trembling with emotion, bore her sentiments. "I want you to disappear from my life so I can forget you." The harsh tone of her voice betrayed her brokenness as she released her clutching fingers from his flesh.

His face paled as he considered her plea. "I agree," he affectionately vocalized. "You are an exceptional woman, and I'm sorry for my participation in this pathetic ploy."

His flattery failed to move her emotions because before her stood the embodiment of a lie.

$$- \cdot \maltese \cdot -$$

A sullen mood hung over the Holland dining table as everyone sipped their soup in silence. Unable to keep her worry contained any longer, Suzette dropped her spoon in the bowl exclaiming her thoughts.

"Where are they? She should be home by now."

"Oh, now you are worried," Philippe mockingly ranted. "It was your idea to allow her to go off alone with the viscount."

The duke raised an arched brow, casting a disgruntled look. "I would appreciate it, sir, if you would not address my wife in such a bold fashion." As he glowered at Philippe's face, he saw it soften.

"I apologize," he quickly countered, "but I am worried sick."

"Understandable, but taking it out on Suzette will serve no purpose." Robert reached out and touched her hand lying limp by the soup bowl.

As they retreated into their silent musings, Robert burst into the room with the driver at his side.

"Is she here?" he yelled, glancing about looking for Jolene.

"No," Philippe answered. He threw his napkin on the side of his plate and rose in haste. "What is he doing here?"

The duke grimaced and rose. Suzette followed suit, bringing her hands to her mouth anticipating terrible news.

"I apologize, Your Grace," the driver began meekly. "But they did not return to the car. I waited for hours and made several inquiries at Hampton Court at closing time, but no one saw them depart."

"What do you mean?" Suzette screeched.

"So you just left?" Philippe shouted.

"All right everyone, calm down," Robert interjected. "You may go, Duncan."

"Thank you." The driver's shoulders slumped as he turned and briskly exited the room.

After his departure, Robert turned mournfully to everyone.

"Sit down," he said. "I have more to tell you."

His mother, trembling at the command, grabbed the duke's hand and sat. Philippe hesitated. His ashen face displayed anxiety.

"The poor driver was afraid to return with the news, so he sought me out at my townhouse first. After he had told me they had disappeared, we departed for the Savoy, looking for the viscount. I had assumed if they had gone anywhere, it would have been back to his hotel."

"I take it they had not arrived," the duke concluded.

"I'm afraid it's worse than that," Robert said, his brow furrowed. "The viscount checked out of the hotel this morning."

"Oh, my God," Suzette cried. "Has she run away with him?"

Philippe frantically interrupted, "He could have kidnapped Jolene."

"Now let's not jump to conclusions because of the past," the duke snapped.

"There is probably the simple explanation that Jolene decided to run away with him," Robert mused. Not convinced of his own conclusion, he feared that something much more sinister may have happened. Why he had checked out of his hotel remained a mystery. "Perhaps his personal affairs came to an end."

"It's all your fault," Suzette asserted, glowering at the men. "You treated him suspiciously and with disrespect. I was the only one who counseled and encouraged her with any kindness. Now look what has happened! She's run away because you rejected him!"

The butler, standing in the doorway, loudly cleared his throat. "Excuse me, my lord, but Mr. Whitefield is here to see you."

Breaking formalities, Alastair burst into the room, his face ruddy with sweat. In his hand he waved an envelope in the air like a flag.

"What are you doing here?" Robert gawked in surprise.

"Grace told me that Jolene didn't come home. Has she returned?" he asked, trying to catch his breath.

"No, she has disappeared." Philippe's voice cracked as he

answered the inquiry.

"I'm afraid I have bad news," Alastair said, brandishing the envelope.

"Good gracious, will you stop waving that infernal thing in my face!" Robert, in his exasperation, snatched it from his hand.

"It's the detective's report," Alastair announced. "Viscount Derrington is an impostor."

"What the hell!" Robert yelled, pulling out the papers. As he opened it, a picture fell to the floor, and Philippe grabbed it.

"You're looking at the real Viscount, who is by all accounts in his eighties. He has no heir. The man purporting to be him is no man of noble birth," Alastair ranted angrily.

Suzette burst into tears, and the duke placed his arm around her to quiet her hysterics. "I think it's time we call the police," he suggested.

"I'll kill that son-of-a-bitch if he's harmed her in any way," Alastair growled.

Philippe lowered his head into the palms of his hands, clearly distraught.

"We will find her," Robert said. "I cannot believe that Jolene would merely disappear and not send word to the family about her whereabouts."

"I hope to God she hasn't run off and married the blackguard," Philippe moaned.

"Or worse," Suzette sniffled. "What if he only means to ruin her?"

Every eye turned in her direction. The duke flashed a warning glare toward Philippe to keep his mouth shut. In response, his eyes narrowed, but he remained silent.

"Send for the police," the duke said. "We shouldn't wait any longer to report her disappearance."

"We'll go," Robert said, looking at Alastair. "Let us take care of it."

"Yes, I'll give them the evidence from the detective." He reached out and retrieved the photograph from Philippe. "There is no time to waste," Alastair said, looking at Robert. "Let's go."

"Don't worry," Robert added, trying to offer comfort to his mother and Philippe. "She has a good head on her shoulders. Let us hope everything turns out all right."

"I've lost my appetite," Philippe grumbled, storming from the room.

Suzette glanced at her husband, who continued to hold her in a comforting embrace.

"Everything will be all right," he encouraged her.

Suzette laid her head on his shoulder and cried.

-·✳·-

Jolene purposely spent the night at the inn alone because it had been part of Geoffrey's plan. James had intended to give her a strong sleeping potion after taking her virginity so she would wake up abandoned. In the morning his benefactor would be waiting for her downstairs to gloat over his victory. Jolene knew that her family would be sick with worry, but the ruse had to be maintained for her own plan to succeed.

After bathing, dressing, and taking her time, she proceeded downstairs. Nervous, yet determined not to let Geoffrey gain the upper hand, she headed for the restaurant.

"Are you Komtesse von Lamberg?" A host approached her in the doorway.

"Yes."

"A gentleman is waiting for you. Follow me," she said.

Jolene inhaled a deep breath, readying herself to play her part in her own devious strategy. As she neared the table, her nervous stomach soured at the sight of Geoffrey. He glanced up and flashed a malevolent smirk, rising to his feet.

"Ah, Komtesse von Lamberg, how good it is to see you again. Won't you have a seat? You must be famished."

"What are you doing here?" Jolene coldly demanded, playing his game. A few heads turned in their direction at the sound of her loud voice.

"I suggest that you take a seat quietly and not make a scene. I'll be happy to tell you exactly what I'm doing here in a few minutes."

Jolene did not protest, but sat in the chair across from Geoffrey, maintaining a controlled demeanor.

"Tea?" he said, pouring her a cup without waiting for an answer. "You look a bit confused," he added. "Looking for James are we?"

After refilling his own cup, he set the pot down.

"Yes," Jolene replied. "What have you done to him?"

Geoffrey snickered. "Oh, that's ripe. What have I done to him? You act as if I've kidnapped the poor man."

"Where is he?" Jolene sternly pressed.

"In Liverpool by now, I would imagine. He has a ship to catch to the Americas in the morning."

"I don't understand." Jolene's voice quavered, continuing her act.

"Well, let me enlighten you then, dearest." Geoffrey smirked. "I paid him two hundred pounds to ruin you. He's decided to spend his newfound fortune on a new life across the big pond, as they call it."

She allowed her mouth to gape open in surprise, but genuine tears welled in her eyes. Even though she had a trick up her sleeve, he had succeeded in piercing her heart with the temptation of love.

"He is no viscount, by the way. He is a commoner from northern England whom I hired to dupe you. Frankly, he did rather well and deserves a bravo for his performance, don't you think?"

A tear trickled down her cheek, and Geoffrey flashed an arrogant, satisfied smile.

"I told you once that you were nothing more than a stuck-up bitch that needed to be knocked down a few notches. When I heard about your visit, I saw the perfect opportunity to get back at you for the cruel denial received in Paris. When James boasted to me of his conquest, it only confirmed that you were an easy whore like your mother."

Jolene stared at him unmoved by his gloating victorious speech. In response, she grinned at him with her confident air that he despised. Her unexpected reaction caught Geoffrey's attention. Slowly she picked up the teacup, took a sip, and then set it down.

"Well, now, isn't that peachy," she began, her eyes sparkling mischievously. "Unfortunately, the ruse is on you."

Tongue-tied, he merely gawked at her, apparently trying to process her proclamation.

"You are an unscrupulous reprobate," she snarled. "And I am most fortunate that you are a poor judge of character. You see," she gloated, "the man you hired had a conscience after all."

"I doubt that," he countered angrily. "He gave me a detailed account, and I paid him the money for ruining your reputation."

She chuckled at his miserable state. "Yes, and I paid Henry Mead another two hundred pounds to lie to your face. He never did the deed."

When he heard Jolene speak his real name, Geoffrey's self-confidence faded. The muscles in his jaw tensed. He glanced at her, roaming his eyes up and down her frame like a lecherous demon.

"I don't believe a word you're saying," he spat. "He said you were tight and sweet."

Even though Jolene could see in his eyes that he questioned her statement, he would not admit defeat.

"We have the room until eleven o'clock," he drawled, reaching out and grabbing her left hand. He squeezed it so tight that she thought her fingers would break. "Why don't we go upstairs and let me find out how tight you really are?"

Jolene's chest heaved angrily after hearing his despicable suggestion. She wanted to pound Geoffrey with her fists. Instead, she picked up a full glass of water and threw it in his face. Gasping in shock, she was able to wrestle her captive hand free from his clutches. Twice in two days, her ability to assault a man had come in handy. Geoffrey grabbed a napkin and wiped his face while the patrons gawked at their interaction.

"Very ladylike," he responded with a chuckle. His disgusting cocky grin returned.

Jolene flung her parting sentiments.

"You are a bloody ass, and I'm sure that Robert and Alastair will have much to say about your latest scheme." As soon as she saw the worried glint in his eyes, she smirked. "I can't wait to find out what they decide to do with you this time."

Rising to her feet, she wanted to spit at him. Her parting

words had evidently brought the fear of consequences, as he pulled his eyes away and began dabbing his wet shirt with the napkin. She retreated and headed for the door, filled with anger and heartbreak.

Yes, he had played her for a fool, but she had just played him for a bigger fool whether he believed it or not.

– · ✳ · –

As planned, Jolene hailed a cab to London and met James at a bank. When she arrived, she caught sight of him standing near the entrance. His demeanor had drastically changed. The confident man who had swept her off her feet looked like a defeated soldier. After asking the driver to wait for a few minutes, she warily approached him.

"Jolene. You came."

"I told you I would," she replied. "I'm sorry that I didn't have the money to pay you last night, but if you give me a few minutes, I will make the withdrawal."

"Of course."

With an aching heart, she tried her best not to let her emotions rule the business at hand. The thoughts of love and brokenness needed to be put aside as she entered the bank. Afterward, she returned with the bills clenched in her palm. James stood by the curb, his shoulders drooping, looking forlorn and lost. She could not imagine him as Henry Mead.

"Here you go," she said, grabbing his hand. She discreetly placed the bills in his palm and stepped back. "Two hundred pounds as we agreed."

"You saw Geoffrey, I take it," he said with interest.

"Yes, we had a rather confrontational conversation regarding the matter." Jolene did not care to elaborate.

"I… I'm sorry, Jolene," he stammered. He lowered his head, averting his gaze. "When this all started, I only thought about my desire for passage to the states. Selfishly I didn't think about the harm it would cause you emotionally."

"And nearly physically," she added with scorn.

"Yes and that." He paused and gazed at her with regret. "I

am glad that things turned out this way, and I hope you can forgive me."

Forgive. Jolene had not the capacity to forgive. Perhaps after they parted, and he boarded a ship bound for another continent, she could forget. Forgiveness would probably never arrive.

"I can't forgive you right now," she painfully admitted, fighting tears. "You broke my heart."

Looking miserably remorseful, he fiddled with the money and then shoved it in his trouser pocket.

"I should go," he announced.

"Then go," she ordered indifferently. Before he stepped away, he leaned in and gave her a quick peck on the cheek.

"Goodbye. You really are a sweet lady."

Jolene closed her eyes, holding back tears. She heard his footsteps fade into the distance and mingle with the crowd of people passing by. When she knew that he had gone, she returned to the cab barely able to breathe.

Her heart had attached itself to a mirage that evaporated before her eyes. She had yearned for love, arrived at its source, and found it to be a cruel joke. With his departure, her dream of marriage vanished.

CHAPTER 20

As the cab pulled into the Holland estate, Jolene dreaded what lay ahead. The entire way back she pondered what to say upon seeing her family, fearing the embarrassing confessions she would need to make. She thought about simply lying about the whole affair, saying they had gone off to lunch and became separated. Perhaps she could tell them she became confused and disoriented in her surroundings and merely took a hotel for the night. Afterward, she would concoct some story about James having to return to York unexpectedly.

As excuse after excuse mulled about in her throbbing head, she came to grips with the harsh reality that she had to admit her terrible mistake. How could she look her mother and father in the eye, let alone Robert, and speak of her private indiscretions? It seemed impossible.

Finally, as the cab slowed and came to a stop, she inhaled a shaky breath. As soon as she exited the car, the door to the front entrance flew open. Robert took one glance at her and ran in her direction. Unable to contain her emotions, her lower lip quivered and tears filled her eyes as she saw the desperation in his eyes.

"Thank God," Robert groaned, gathering her in his arms.

She peered over her shoulder and saw Alastair, looking pale but relieved. Robert embraced her so tightly she thought her ribs would crack.

"Are you all right? Did he hurt you?" He eyed her frame up

and down.

"No," she sheepishly answered, lowering her head in shame.

"He is not who he says he is, Jolene," Alastair said, approaching the two of them. "The man is an impostor."

"I know," she sniffled. The sordid tale lay heavily upon her heart. She looked back and forth at their anxious faces, waiting for her to continue with her explanation.

"How do you know?" Robert asked. "Did he admit to his reprehensible actions?"

"Yes, well, no," Jolene said, biting her lower lip. She did not wish to blame Henry entirely, so she turned their attention to the culprit. "Geoffrey Chambers…"

"Geoffrey Chambers?" bellowed Alastair. "What the hell does he have to do with it?"

Speaking Geoffrey's name incited such ire in both Robert's and Alastair's eyes, Jolene clamped her mouth shut. She hated him as much as anyone else but had no desire to expose the reason for his involvement. It would implicate her and reveal the fact she had nearly fallen victim to his ruinous plan. A knot formed in her stomach as they continued to stare at her, apparently waiting for her to expound upon the statement. She wrapped her hand around her waist.

"He hired James—his real name is Henry—to dupe me," she admitted. "Please, I beg you, not to pressure me for more. As you can see, I am fine," she said, desperately attempting to lift her lips into a small smile. "Mother and Father must be terribly worried. Are they here?"

"Worried is not the word I would use," Robert informed her. "More like hysterical. Philippe is convinced you have been kidnapped again."

"Oh, poor man," Jolene said. "I am so very sorry." Her eyes shifted to Alastair, whose agitation had grown tenfold by the look of his dark eyes and clenched fists. His lips clamped in a straight line as if to prevent himself from letting out a stream of ungentlemanly curses.

By the gaze in their eyes, she knew they wondered if she had given herself to Henry before knowing the truth of his identity. The anxious thoughts ruminating in her mind about what to say next were short-lived when the remainder of the family charged toward her.

As soon as she saw her father's angry face, she expected another squabble to ensue between the two of them. Thankfully, her mother appeared greatly relieved, bracing her tightly.

"Thank God you are all right," she sighed. "We were so worried about you."

Her loving and nonjudgmental tone put Jolene at ease. Of course she understood. Philippe, however, unable to smile with relief, glowered at her harshly.

"Yes, we were worried sick," her father spoke. "I am glad you are home safe and sound." He gave her a perfunctory, short hug.

The duke appeared in the doorway and nodded his head. "I see you have safely returned," he commented, flashing a relieved smile. "Why don't you come in and have a relaxing cup of tea. The time for tears and worry are over."

Tea? A cup was the last thing on Jolene's mind. She glanced at everyone standing around waiting for a detailed blow-by-blow description of her foolhardiness.

"That sounds delightful, but I'm afraid I am exhausted. If you will be so kind to excuse me, I would rather retire to my room."

Jolene did not wait for any protests. She modestly slipped by everyone and crossed the threshold without a glance backward, sprinting up the staircase to her room. Once inside, she closed the door and heaved a relieved sigh. In all her haste, she had forgotten to apologize to anyone in her family for putting them through such distress. If she had learned anything in the past two days about her personality, it was that she proved to be untrustworthy, weak willed, and could lie to save face. After the harsh realization of the depths she had sunken, she proceeded to weep unabashedly in self-pity.

— ·❈· —

"So that's it?" Philippe snidely remarked. "No explanation for her whereabouts. No apologies for disappearing overnight.

She merely runs off and says she is tired." He huffed in exasperation. "Forget the tea. I need a drink." Philippe stormed past the duke into the foyer, heading for the parlor.

Suzette ignored Philippe's tirade and turned her attention to her son. "What did she say? Anything?"

"Nothing of consequence, frankly. She discovered the viscount was a fraud," he answered back. "I think she's far too embarrassed to elaborate about the time they spent together. I can only speculate."

"Oh, dear," Suzette said.

"Would you like a drink too?" The duke smirked.

"I know I would," Robert chimed in return. "Alastair, what about you?"

"Thank you, but I have business to attend to," he said with a solemn face. "Jolene is home and safe. That's all the matters."

"Understandable. I will give you a call in the morning, ole chap." Robert gave him a pat on the arm and turned to follow his parents indoors.

When he walked into the parlor, Philippe sat sulking in a chair staring into a glass of alcohol. His father headed for the decanter, and Robert followed close behind.

"Nothing for me," Suzette said. "I really think I should go talk to Jolene."

"Yes, why don't you," Philippe quipped. "I dislike not knowing what happened to her in the past two days."

"I wouldn't pressure her too much," Robert interjected. "She may not be ready to talk."

"Nonsense," Suzette objected. "Mothers can have the discussions you gentlemen cannot, and I think you know what I mean."

Philippe's brows arched. "Do you think they... you know..." Philippe couldn't articulate the obvious.

"Had relations?" Robert replied. "I'm not sure, but I'll bet you the alleged viscount got exactly what he wanted at Geoffrey Chambers's prodding."

"What are you talking about?" the duke said, scowling. "What does that ass have to do with this entire fiasco?"

"I'm not entirely sure, but I have a sneaking suspicion the

business Alastair is about to take care of will reveal the answer to that question."

Robert took a gulp and settled back into the chair. He was not too worried about sensible Alastair doing anything rash, except for shouting at Geoffrey. There had never been a time when Robert witnessed Alastair fly into an uncontrollable rage. Convinced his friend only intended to dish out a verbal lashing, he decided not to worry about it.

–·✳·–

Suzette let the words between the three men drift into the distance as she walked down the hall. With Jolene's room in the far wing of the estate, it would give her time to gather her fragmented thoughts. Relieved she had safely returned, there remained an obvious question. What happened yesterday? What happened last night? She shuddered at the conversation ahead but decided to tread cautiously around the subject.

When she reached Jolene's suite, she vacillated for a second, then softly rapped on the door. Jolene's shaky voice replied.

"Yes, who is it?"

"It's your mother, dearest. Might I come in?" Suzette expected her daughter instantly to respond but instead heard silence, which clearly indicated Jolene's hesitancy to talk. "I promise not to badger you," Suzette assured her softly. A moment later, the door opened. Jolene appeared with a red nose and swollen eyes.

"Oh dear," Suzette said, slipping past her daughter and closing the door. "You definitely need comfort." She slipped her arms around her daughter, who did not protest. As the tears began to pour again, Suzette merely patted her softly on the back. "I'm sorry he broke your heart."

After a few sniffles and wiping her nose with her hankie, Jolene looked at her forlornly.

"I'm not sure if it's a broken heart I nurse or the anger I harbor that he has taken me for such a fool."

Jolene turned away, walked toward the edge of her bed, and sat down. "I have been so imprudent, Mother." Her face reddened with emotion.

For a few seconds Suzette let her expel her pent-up emotions, listening to her heartbreaking cries.

"Do you want to talk about what happened, or shall I leave you to your thoughts to work through the pain?"

Suzette did not mean to pressure her, but on the other hand, the looming question of lost virginity would not go away. Consequences were bound to happen to her family and friends if the truth got out, not to mention the danger of pregnancy. She wrung her hands together in a worrisome act which Jolene noticed.

"Don't go," she whispered. "We should talk, but I beg you not to speak with Father, Robert, or anyone else about what I'm going to tell you."

Suzette sat down in a chair next to the bed and took Jolene's cold hands into hers. "You have my word whatever passes between us will stay in this room."

After another sniffle, Jolene looked up. Her eyes were filled with sadness and not shame.

"I loved him. He swept me off my feet and told me he had fallen in love with me." Jolene paused. "But he is a scoundrel!"

"Apparently so."

"In seeking privacy, we left the driver and grounds." She thought for a moment. "You didn't fire the poor man on my account did you?"

"No, he's still in our employ," Suzette answered.

"Good. I would feel dreadful if you had because James had thought of the scheme. I agreed to his suggestion."

The devilish rogue apparently had the entire thing planned ahead of time, Suzette thought. "Where did he take you?"

"To an inn just outside the gates and down the street. We only went for something to eat, but then… then he suggested we get a room."

Suzette's stomach tightened at the thought of what must have happened next. Why did she go with him? Of course, she knew the answer to that question more than anyone else did after begging Robert to take her the first time.

"He paid for a room, and I joined him. One thing led to

another and…"

"Did you give yourself to him?" Suzette reached out and tenderly wrapped her hand around her daughter's forearm. Unexpectedly, Jolene's tears turned into a giggle that continued for a few seconds. Stupefied over her actions, Suzette asked again. "Well did you?"

"Well, for a few minutes he tried his best to entice me to lay with him, but when he became a bit aggressive, all I could see was Geoffrey Chambers's face in front of me, and that terrible incident with him came flooding back."

"Oh, dear."

"So I slapped him hard across the face, and he immediately stopped."

"Good for you," Suzette exclaimed. A weight lifted from her shoulders.

"Oh, Mother, after that everything fell apart. He confessed to me Geoffrey Chambers had paid him to seduce and ruin me."

As Suzette's mouth gaped open in utter surprise, she felt her heart beat thunderously against her ribcage. "That conniving little…" She held her tongue not wishing to swear in front of her daughter, but her mind raged with multiple French obscenities.

"Reprobate?" Jolene finished her sentence. "Don't worry about it, Mother, because the joke is really on him."

"How?"

"I paid James—well, his name is really Henry—a few more pounds to tell Geoffrey he had succeeded."

"Why in the world did you do that?" By the blank look in her eyes, it didn't appear Jolene had thought it through.

"Because I wanted to turn the tables on Geoffrey and gloat over him in return."

"So the young man agreed, I take it."

"Yes, by now he's on a train to Liverpool to catch a ship to the Americas. Frankly, I wanted him gone and out of my life, I suppose."

Suzette considered her daughter's actions, keenly aware that she had fallen desperately in love.

"I'm so very sorry he broke your heart."

Her daughter whimpered, and tears welled again in her eyes.

"I suppose he did, but it wasn't real. It was a façade. The man held no real affection for me."

"Yes, but thankfully he didn't pressure you and eventually spoke the truth. I do suppose that is one good quality about him."

"He wanted my forgiveness, but I couldn't grant it," Jolene admitted.

"But what of Geoffrey? I don't understand why you let him think he got away with it at first?"

"He waited for me this morning at the hotel café, and I just let him gloat. Then I revealed the truth to him. At first I don't think he believed me until I spoke James's real name."

"Then what?" Suzette leaned forward interested for the next tidbit.

"He suggested we go upstairs and have sex, so I threw a full glass of water in his face."

"You did?" Suzette's eyes widened. "A bit unladylike in public but deserving, I should say." The unveiling of Geoffrey's involvement in the affair boiled Suzette's blood. "That boy is such a reprobate," Suzette shrieked. "So help me, I'll see to it he's driven out of the country if I have any say in it. Wait until my husband hears of this or Robert for that matter. There will be hell to pay."

A slow smirk curled Jolene's lips. "Mother, I never imagined you could get so angry."

"As the English would say, I bloody well am." Suzette let out a few French curse words Jolene recognized, and she giggled. The levity brought her anger under control, and Suzette gave her daughter a tight hug.

"Be of good cheer, my dearest, that Geoffrey's plan failed. Your heart will heal and some wonderful man will fall in love with you and all will be well again."

"My reputation in England will be ruined, if Geoffrey starts to spread the word. Perhaps, I should just go back to Vienna."

"No, not yet," Suzette said. "I won't let you leave so soon. We will make this right. Don't worry about it." She hesitated. "Besides, Robert's wedding is coming up and you don't want to miss that, now do you?"

"Oh, dear, I almost forgot."

"I'm glad he's settling down," Suzette said, thinking fondly of him. "Grace is such a wonderful girl."

"Yes, she is."

"And her brother is quite nice too, don't you think?"

Jolene raised a brow and looked at her mother's obvious point.

"Yes, Alastair is a very nice man, but I have made a mess of things," she groaned.

As terrible as it looked to her daughter, Suzette felt assured all would turn out as it should.

CHAPTER 21

Alastair locked the door to his bedroom suite and dashed across to the other side. In a frenzied motion, he grabbed the handle to his closet, flung it open, and reached to the shelf above his head. Red-faced and burning with anger, he searched for the box. Unable to find it, he frantically tossed his belongings to the floor. At last the wooden case emerged, and Alastair snatched it from its hiding place.

His heart pounded heatedly as he held the custom walnut case and considered the contents. Some time ago he purchased the item for display but never felt inclined to carry a weapon—at least not until today. He rubbed his hand along the wood grain and wiped away the dust. Inside lay a 1908 vest pocket Colt automatic pistol, which was more than adequate to do the job.

Walking over to his writing table, he sat down and opened the lid. The casing of metal gun shimmered from the streaming light of his desk lamp. Alastair carefully pulled out the nickel-plated firearm by the ivory grip. His hand shook as he fingered the trigger. It would only take one shot to end the sordid affair.

He laid the gun on the tabletop and examined the contents of the box. It contained the manufacturer's cleaning tools, an empty magazine, and fifty-four .25-caliber bullets placed point down in round holes. The interior lid of the case included written instructions. Alastair briefly scanned the document until he felt confident in handling the weapon.

Picking up the magazine, he opened the metal closure and then methodically removed six bullets. One by one he placed them in the metal container and then closed it shut. With force, he shoved it into the bottom grip of the gun and pushed it upward until it clicked. The firearm, no bigger than the palm of his hand, lay on his cold flesh, loaded and ready to hit its target.

He jolted when hearing a loud pounding on his door.

"Alastair, let me in!"

"Go away, Grace," he growled. "I have nothing to say." After three more pounds of his sister's fist, she bellowed again.

"Let me in before you do something rash," she howled.

"Rash?" He rose from his chair and strode with heavy footsteps toward the door. In his right hand he clutched the loaded gun. "Do you think we should stand by and do nothing after what *he* has done to her?" His body trembled as he screamed his livid response.

"Alastair, let me in," Grace moaned, lowering her voice in a tearful plea.

With his chest constricting in rage, he knew he had to shut her up or she would awaken the entire household. Her pounding heightened his agitated state.

With his cold left hand, Alastair reached forward and turned the metal doorknob. Grace, surprised at his surrender, stood stiffly on the other side of the threshold. Her reddened face matched the color of her lipstick. When she glanced at his stance and noticed the gun clutched in his right hand, she gasped aloud.

"What are you doing with that gun?"

"It's none of your business," he barked. Alastair's eyes grew dark. His soul hardened with disdain. He'd never felt such an urge to stop a wicked, beating heart in the chest of a man as he did at that moment. Besides, without her, his life held no value. The gallows would be sufficient to ease his emotional pain and well worth the spectacle of watching a blackguard die at his feet.

"Where are you going?" Grace pitched forward and grabbed his arm.

"Out of my way," he demanded with clenched teeth. In a quick jerk he pulled free of her grasp and headed for the door.

"No, Alastair! Don't do this!"

He would hear none of her pleas. Swiftly he ran down the stairs and heard the frantic footsteps of Grace follow closely behind. As he reached the front entrance and swung the door open, she clutched his arm tightly with both hands, digging her nails into the sleeve of his coat.

"I beg of you, don't do something you'll regret," she cried. Frightful tears moistened her eyes.

Alastair gazed into his sister's horrified countenance. "Let me go, Grace, before I am forced to hurt you." It deeply pained his heart having to threaten her, but she needed to stop and leave him to carry out his intent.

Astonished at his words, she quickly released him and stepped backward. Grace brought her hands to her mouth, trembling over his threat. Alastair said nothing more and walked into the night, hell-bent on killing the vilest human being on earth.

Geoffrey returned to his modest flat at dusk. He kicked off his shoes, threw his topcoat on a chair, rid himself of his tie, and unbuttoned his shirt. After pouring an ample amount of whiskey into a glass, he flopped on his divan and got comfortable. It had been a good day—a damn good day. He was on top of the world, in spite of the fact he had been living in less than comfortable accommodations than he had been used to in the past.

After the Paris fiasco, his father kicked him out of the house to appease the duke. Frankly, he did not give a damn. With the generous allowance that his father still provided at his mother's urging, he made his rent, had food on the table, and a few extra bobs to gamble with and buy liquor. Plenty of women came and went to satisfy his sexual appetites, and he occasionally enjoyed the little wench who liked it rough at the brothel.

When he heard the komtesse was returning on holiday, he began his elaborate plan to ruin the bitch. He should have done the deed himself while in Paris. Unfortunately, his cousin had to come to the rescue. The affair strained family relationships and affected his friendship with Alastair. Frankly, he didn't miss

Robert or Alastair, because he had found new friends more akin to his lifestyle. Geoffrey lived his life as he damn well pleased according to his code of conduct.

Finding someone to play the rogue with Jolene had been easy after he inquired in a few unscrupulous social circles. The man came highly recommended, and after investing a few crowns in the lad's appearance, he had pulled off exactly what he wanted.

Yet things did not quite go as he had planned. Frankly, he did not know whether to believe Jolene, who he thought merely tried to save face by denying his cohort had done the deed. Rather than wrestling with the possibility he had failed, he decided to believe she lied. A plausible explanation could be behind Henry confessing his name for his own amusement afterward. He chose to believe another version rather than the far-fetched story she claimed.

As he pondered the affair, a loud rap jolted the door to his flat. He set down his drink on a table and rose to his feet. The insistent pounding continued.

"All right, all right," he bellowed. "I'm coming." Thinking perhaps it was one of his drunken mates looking for a place to sleep it off, Geoffrey threw open the door. What greeted him on the other side was not what he expected. He gasped and instinctively stepped backward as his eyes met the barrel of a Colt revolver with Alastair Whitefield's finger on the trigger.

"Get your ass back inside, you degenerate."

"What kind of greeting is that for your ole friend," Geoffrey nervously chortled. "Why don't you put that thing down? I don't appreciate the view."

Alastair did not respond except to shove the door behind him shut. He kept advancing with the gun in hand, and Geoffrey kept retreating. When he reached the seat of a chair, he had nowhere further to go except on his ass. He plopped on the seat, hoping the gun would retreat. Instead, Alastair kept it pointed at his skull only a few inches from his head.

"You son-of-a-bitch," he began to rail at him. "You fucking bastard. You don't deserve to live another second."

Geoffrey cringed and with a trembling voice responded. "I guess you discovered my little ploy with Jolene, did you? Bloody brilliant, don't you think?"

"I'm going to kill you, Chambers," Alastair snarled. "I'm going to rid the world of your kind."

"If you do, you'll swing at the end of a rope. Who will save Jolene's reputation then? You think anyone will marry that whore after fucking a nobody from Liverpool?" As fearful as Geoffrey felt under the scrutiny of a Colt pistol, he could not help but taunt Alastair. He thought about putting up a fight, but Alastair had always been taller and stronger. His trigger finger would probably pull back at the first attempt and splatter his brains on the wall. Things were not looking good.

"Why would you go out of your way to ruin her? For what purpose?"

The gun came closer until the barrel touched his skull. Geoffrey felt Alastair's hand tremble.

"I thought she was a stuck-up bitch, that's why, and needed to be taken down a notch. The woman is insufferable," he said. It was impossible not to grin. "I enjoyed seeing her fall in grace. She's a whore, like her mother, and if you can't see that, then you're blind."

Alastair released a laughed, which sounded sinister as hell. "Whore? What a joke. You're riding them every night, and you think she's a whore? She's a victim and nothing more."

"Go ahead, pull the trigger if it makes you feel any better. Rid society of one more bloody sod." His voice was flat and unwavering. After his invitation to Alastair to go through with it, he waited. Instead, he heard the door to the apartment fly open and frantic footsteps stomp across the room.

"Alastair, put the gun down."

It was his cousin, Robert. Geoffrey held his breath. This time he had come to rescue his ass. How ironic.

"I don't want to," Alastair responded with a growl. "Do you think he has the right to live?" He pressed the barrel against his head harder.

"If you shoot him, it will ruin your life. Do not give that asshole the satisfaction he's won again if he's rotting in hell. He'll probably have a drink with Lucifer himself and laugh that he brought you down too."

"I probably would," Geoffrey agreed with a nervous laugh. Alastair pressed the barrel harder. "I hate him."

"As do I, but killing him will only ruin you," Robert pleaded.

"Your cousin will probably represent you in court and call it a crime of passion," Geoffrey said. "Maybe he can save you from the hangman's noose."

"Shut the bloody hell up," Robert barked. He turned toward Alastair, pleading again.

"Put the gun down. We can always give him a good punch and break his damn nose. What say you, friend? Let's just screw up his face a bit and leave him to wallow in pain."

"Now wait a minute, cousin," Geoffrey protested looking up. When he did, he saw a relieved smile curl Alastair's lips.

"Sounds good to me," he said, pulling the gun away and slipping it back in his waistcoat pocket. "Why don't you hold him while I rearrange that nose of his?"

Robert's hands landed on Geoffrey's shoulders keeping him firmly planted in the chair.

"I'll file charges if you hit me. You'll still go to jail for assault!" He screamed, trying to dodge the blow. It was too late because the next thing he remembered was a giant fist coming straight toward his nose. He heard the bones crush underneath Alastair's knuckles and felt blood spurt from his nostrils.

"I'm satisfied now," Alastair said, shaking off the hard whack from his hand. "He should have two black eyes by the morning."

"You fucking bastard," Geoffrey railed, holding his nose with both hands. "You broke my damn nose!"

"Be thankful he didn't blow your head off," Robert reminded him.

"I'll file charges," Geoffrey cried. "You won't get away with this." He wailed in pain like a pig. "Son-of-a-bitch!"

"I doubt anyone will believe you. As far as the two of us are concerned, we were never here."

Robert grabbed Alastair by the upper arm. "Come on, mate, let's go have a drink."

Geoffrey watched as the two of them exited his flat and slammed the door behind them.

"Fuck," he screamed, holding his bleeding nose. He had never felt so much pain in his entire life.

— · ✳ · —

As soon as Alastair and Robert stepped outdoors, Robert turned toward his friend to give him a harsh lecture. "What the hell did you think you were doing?"

"Giving the man a broken nose," he said nonchalantly, rubbing his knuckles.

"How long have you had that Colt?"

"What this?" Alastair replied, shoving his hand into his pocket and retrieving it.

"Let me have that, you fool," Robert said, snatching it from his hand. He looked at the gun handle and realized there was no magazine. "Where are the bullets?"

"Here." Alastair stuck his hand in the pocket of his trousers and retrieved the case.

"You mean it wasn't loaded?"

"Well, it was when I left the house," he admitted. "But by the time I arrived, I decided I didn't want to hang for killing the no-good ass. I had intended on the broken nose all along after I scared the daylights out of him and hoped he would piss his trousers while looking down the barrel of a gun." Alastair laughed. "He's probably pissing them now!"

Robert handed the weapon back. "You bugger," he railed. "Grace came over in a hysterical panic, crying you had left to kill him. When she told me you had a gun in hand, your intention appeared obvious."

"After all these years you actually thought I could blow his brains out?"

"Well, you must admit, passion can make a man do irrational things." Robert countered.

"For goodness' sake, my conscience pricks me when I smash a fly." He rubbed his sore hand again. "It felt pretty damn good though, feeling his nasal bones crush beneath my fist. I don't think I'll ever forget the sensation."

"I need a drink," Robert moaned.

"Me too," Alastair said. "To our favorite pub?"

"Hell yes," Robert said, throwing his arm around Alastair's shoulder. "I don't know what I would do without you. You're one hell of a man."

"So the ladies tell me." Alastair smirked. "So the ladies tell me."

CHAPTER 22

"Are you doubting my word, Detective?" The duke lifted his head and narrowed his eyes, displaying his displeasure over the "are you sure" question from the stout officer standing in their parlor.

The detective glanced around at the family audience, peering at him with glaring eyes. "Of course not. I wouldn't think of it," he said, returning his notepad to his pocket. "If your son and Mr. Whitefield were both here last evening, I'm sure it was for good reason."

Alastair saw Grace take a step forward and wrap her arm around Robert's, hanging limply at his side. He worried about her saying something that would put them at risk.

"There certainly was a good reason, officer. It was our engagement dinner party." She pursed her lips showing her displeasure over the accusation. "Certainly you would not dare to tarnish an important event in my life by such unfounded accusations." Her lip quivered for effect.

"No, no, I wouldn't think of it," he said, shuffling his feet. "Well then, I will speak with Mr. Chambers that you deny any involvement."

"The man often gets into drunken brawls at the local pub and forgets who hit him last," Robert interjected. "Frankly, he's the black sheep of the family, if you get my drift."

"Oh, I do. I have done some of my own investigation

regarding the man's character and have heard about his questionable behavior around town." He nodded in deference to the duke. "If you will excuse me, Your Grace, I will take my leave."

"Of course, Detective Wallace," the duke replied. "Enjoy your evening."

"Good evening," Suzette added.

Alastair stood motionless with everyone else in the room. He held his breath, feeling his heart pounding in his chest. When they were assured that the detective had departed and the doors to the parlor were securely shut, everyone sighed in relief.

"Well, that was entertaining," Philippe chimed in.

"It frightened me," Jolene said. "Thankfully, he believed us."

"I have an announcement to make," the duke said, changing the subject. "I'm sure that all of you will be delighted."

"What is it?" the duchess glanced at him curiously.

"My sister sent word today that her husband has cut Geoffrey's allowance off. She, of course, is severely distressed. Rather than choosing overt poverty, it appears at his father's insistence, Geoffrey will be enlisting in the Royal Navy."

"Good Lord, you must be kidding?" Robert roared. "Geoffrey on the high seas? He will be vomiting his guts out for months."

"How comical," Alastair added. "Robert is quite right. The slightest motion even in a row boat, and the man turns green as a frog."

"Fitting end," Philippe agreed with a broad smile.

"I am afraid my sister is beside herself," the duke added. "She begged Lord Chambers to purchase Geoffrey a commission in the Royal Regiment of his choice, but he refused."

"Well, what a surprising turn of events for Lord Chambers to act with an ounce of decency. I didn't think he had it in him," Suzette commented. "Did you have anything to do with it?"

"Oh, I may have put in a word or two," he remarked.

"Well, I must be off," Alastair announced, putting his drink down on the table. "Your Grace, thank you for saving me from an embarrassing situation."

"My pleasure, Alastair. Some men are meant to be saved while others aren't worth the effort."

"Grace, you coming with me?" he asked. Of course he knew full well she would hang on Robert's arm for at least another hour or two.

"Not yet," she moaned.

"I'll return her home," Robert said.

"At a decent hour too, or your nose will be next," he said, shaking his index finger in Robert's face.

Everyone in the room chuckled. He glanced at Jolene and bowed his head. "Komtesse."

Though the outcome had been a favorable one, being near Jolene only reminded him of the yearning for her love. The ache never left. After Robert's wedding, she would probably return to Vienna, forgetting about him altogether.

As the butler helped him on with his overcoat in the foyer, to his surprise Jolene appeared.

"Alastair, can I have a word?"

Surprised, he waited for privacy and answered. "Yes, what is it?"

"What fist did you use to punch him?"

Slightly shocked by the question, he stood there momentarily, looking at Jolene with a befuddled expression. "Why, this one," he said, lifting up a clenched right hand.

Jolene stepped forward and cupped her palms around his flesh. Unexpectedly, she softly kissed his bruised knuckles. Alastair watched speechless at her show of affection.

"Thank you for defending my honor, Alastair. I am deeply indebted."

The sincerity in her eyes moved him. "You are most welcome, but you need not thank me."

"I owe you an apology."

"For what?"

"For the insincere apology that I gave you the last time we were alone." Her voice quavered. "I am truly sorry for how I treated you in light of recent events. I frankly deserved it."

Taken aback by her words, Alastair felt tongue-tied to respond. The tone of her voice and trembling hold of his hand convinced him she meant every word.

"Apology accepted," he whispered, pulling away from her grasp. Her touch, even now, aroused every nerve ending in his body.

"I wish I could make it up to you," Jolene said, looking into his eyes forlornly. "But I don't suppose you would care to have a woman like myself at your side now." Appearing embarrassed, she pulled her eyes away and looked downward. "I want you to know nothing happened between the fake viscount and myself— though he did try."

Alastair's heart pounded with anticipation against his ribcage. Had she changed her mind about him?

"I think nothing less of you, Jolene, if that is what you are concerned about. You were the victim in this terrible ploy of deceit. I suppose if the situation had been reversed, I might have done the same."

Her brow over her right eye rose high. "You mean if a woman seduced you? Do women really do such things?"

It did sound a bit absurd, Alastair thought. Nevertheless, even though she was guilty of nearly succumbing, her question revealed an untainted innocence that remained.

"I'm not sure, frankly. I have never been approached by any woman in such a way."

"If there is anything I can ever do to show you my heartfelt gratitude, just name it," Jolene offered.

"Dinner might help." His response came quickly and with purpose. "Might I pick you up Friday evening at seven thirty?"

"Are you sure you want to be seen with me in public?" Jolene said in a sad voice.

"I would be proud to have you by my side." He reached for her hand and kissed it gently. "If anyone dares to judge, there may be more broken noses around London."

Jolene smiled. "All right, seven thirty Friday."

"I look forward to it." Alastair nodded his head and left.

Jolene swung around to see Robert standing at the far end of the foyer with a skeptical look on his face.

"Don't toy with him," he said, taking a step in her direction. "I don't think he could handle another heartbreak."

"I promise not to," Jolene responded. "I will be honest and will not lead him on."

"Is it gratitude or curiosity?" Robert inquired.

"A bit of both, I think. Now that I've pushed the foolish side of my heart aside, perhaps I can experience the wiser."

"Perhaps," he replied warily.

"I am terribly sorry for how I have acted, Robert. I owe you an apology too for being so bullheaded."

"Yes, you are bullheaded," he chuckled. "Apology accepted."

"Thank goodness you arrived in time to keep Alastair from killing Geoffrey. I would have never forgiven myself if he had gone too far."

"Well, he came to his senses long before I arrived, but he did enjoy breaking Geoffrey's big nose."

Grace entered the foyer and joined them. "So, what am I missing?"

"Apparently, my half sister has a dinner engagement with your brother this Friday. Should I let her go?"

Grace's eyes widened, and she glanced suspiciously at Jolene. "Do be kind to him," she firmly pleaded. "He has a good heart."

"I know," Jolene agreed. "I promise. Truly, I do."

"Well, then that settles it," Grace said. "Robert, take me for a walk in the garden. I need a kiss under the moonlight."

Robert rolled his eyes. "See what she puts me through?" he balked, as Grace dragged him toward the door. "I blame you for this."

Jolene shook her head. "As if you're suffering." She laughed. He flashed a wicked grin in response, and the two of them disappeared into the dark. A sigh escaped Jolene's lungs, thinking about how lucky they were to be in love. She, on the other hand, had been in love with an illusion. Without the substance of truth, the emotion swiftly died, leaving a gaping hole in her heart.

"All you all right?" Her loving mother came to her side. "I suspect Grace and Robert are off exchanging kisses in the garden together."

"Yes, they are."

"She is such a sweet girl. They make a lovely couple," her mother said wistfully. "I wish them all the happiness."

"Yes, they are lucky."

"And what of you, dear? Did you have words with Alastair?"

"Yes, I apologized again."

"He wasn't harsh with you was he?"

"No, always the perfect gentleman," Jolene replied. "He asked me out to dinner, and I accepted."

"Well now, that is a change in direction. Are you sure that is wise based on your lack of affection for him?"

Jolene lowered her head. "I promised Robert that I wouldn't play with his feelings, and I don't intend to. But I need to know."

"Know what?"

"If I could fall in love with him," she grinned.

"Well, if you haven't noticed by now, Alastair is smitten. The poor man can barely breathe or talk when he stands near you."

"After what I've done, I'm surprised he still wishes to be with me."

Suzette took her daughter's hand. "Men in love are strange creatures. As a woman, you should take advantage of his inability to act rationally."

"I'll keep that in mind when I want something." She giggled.

Robert and Grace strolled back into the estate hand in hand. It was impossible not to grin over Grace's hairstyle in disarray and lipstick on Robert's lips.

"What have you two been up to?" Suzette teasingly inquired.

"We only took a stroll in the garden," Robert said, passing her on the way to the parlor.

Grace giggled and quickly tried to push back a few hairpins falling out of her hairdo.

"Shall we join them?" Jolene asked.

"We should. I'm not sure how long your father can keep up a civil conversation with the duke, but they do seem to be getting along better."

They had been too, which made Jolene happy. The thought of having to leave for Vienna in the not-too-distant future upset her peaceful state of mind. After Robert married, decisions would have to be made. She would worry about them tomorrow.

Chapter 23

Even though she had been in Alastair's presence often, she felt nervous about their dinner date. No one seemed to mind she was going out for dinner unchaperoned with him. Of course, Alastair could do no wrong in the eyes of the Hollands. Even her father worshipped him after the nose-breaking incident.

Unfortunately though, Jolene's relationship with Philippe had become strained after the recent affair. Though she had not overtly admitted to her indiscretion to him, he acted as if he surmised as much. Her mother had kept her word not to discuss the private events. Nevertheless, Jolene believed her actions only served to irritate old wounds regarding her mother. Jolene hoped that eventually her father would forgive her foolishness.

As she took one last glance at herself in the mirror, a soft knock came at her bedroom door. Her mother's voice announced Alastair's arrival.

"Mr. Whitefield is in the parlor waiting for you, Jolene."

She opened the door to greet Suzette, who immediately scanned her attire.

"You're dressed rather conservatively this evening," she mused.

"Do you think?" Jolene replied, looking down at her plain green skirt. When she walked over and glanced at herself in the mirror again, she did look rather dowdy in appearance. "It's a drab color," she replied.

"Why don't you wear your purple silk gown? At least it brings out the color in your cheeks. This one looks like you want to blend into the shrubbery and disappear." Her mother walked to the closet and began pushing dresses aside until she found a better alternative.

"The neckline is a bit low. I feel like a hussy, and this makes me feel worse," Jolene moaned.

"Well, buttoning a dress up to your chin is a bit of an overstatement, don't you think?" Suzette laid the dress on the bed. "Why don't you change, and I'll tell Alastair you will be down in a few minutes."

Jolene did not protest. A low neckline had never bothered her before, but now she felt exposed and half naked. She had no qualms about catching her heartbreaking viscount with her bodice, but Alastair was a different type of man.

After changing, Jolene made her way downstairs. She found Alastair conversing with her father alone in the parlor. When she entered, Philippe ceased his conversation.

"Excuse me," he said, quickly slipping from their company.

Alastair appeared confused by his actions.

"I'm afraid he has not forgiven me for my indiscretions," she admitted. She paused for a second and lowered her gaze. "Frankly, I am not sure if I have forgiven myself."

"Let's not worry about that tonight," Alastair sweetly replied. "Tonight it is dinner between the two of us and has nothing to do with the past."

Relieved by his answer, Jolene smiled. "I like that idea."

"Well then, shall we?"

He offered her his arm and escorted her out-of-doors. She expected a sedan and driver to be waiting with an open door. However, to her surprise, a new sports car sat in the drive. Jolene thought it quite unnatural for the situation.

"Is this yours?" A red roadster with white rim wheels and gold trimming met her eyes.

"You don't mind, do you? I confess I adore my snazzy roadster." He grinned.

"No, I don't mind. I'm surprised, that's all." He held the door open for her, and she climbed into the compartment and sat on the white leather seat.

"I'm not really the bore you think I am," he said, laughing at her surprised expression. "I do have eclectic interests."

He shut her door and then climbed in behind the steering wheel. Alastair started the engine, which sounded like a purring lion.

"You better hang on, young lady." He put the car in gear, and pressed the gas pedal, sending small rocks flying into the air behind them. Jolene grabbed Alastair's arm out of fright and giggled as they sped down the drive.

After an exhilarating trip, they finally arrived at their destination. Alastair had chosen a rather out-of-the-way restaurant, which afforded them a more private atmosphere than a busy dining venue in the city.

"The food is excellent, even though it's not a posh London restaurant," he explained, almost sounding apologetic. "I prefer a bit more privacy. However, if you mind, we can go elsewhere."

Still dealing with a tinge of embarrassment being in his presence, Jolene had no objection. "No, I don't mind at all," she replied, scanning the menu. Their orders were placed, and the waiter poured Jolene a glass of wine that Alastair had ordered. Her mind wandered back to her recent heartbreak. A pang of disappointment brought a frown to her face.

"Not to your liking?" Alastair inquired as she continued silently to ponder the glass on the table.

"No, it's fine. The drink brought back unpleasant thoughts," she admitted.

By the sour expression on Alastair's face, it was obvious he knew exactly what she thought about.

"I sometimes think a broken nose wasn't enough punishment for Geoffrey. It's a shame the imposter couldn't have taken his trip to the Americas with a broken nose as well," he confessed in an extremely agitated tone.

Jolene sipped her wine, keeping her gaze averted from his face.

"I almost paid a terrible price to experience passion." Jolene had not meant to say aloud what she inwardly pondered. Nevertheless, her thoughts slipped from between her lips as another confession that begged his forgiveness. Why did she feel like she had to continually confess her sins to Alastair? If she kept it up, she would ruin their evening together. She was supposed to forget about the past, but it clung to her like a prickly weed.

Alastair remained quiet, pondering her words. When Jolene found the courage to lift her eyes and look at him, he spoke.

"I agree passion has a price," he began somberly. In a show of overt affection, he reached across the table and took her limp hand in his. "But passion also has its rewards."

Mesmerized by his declaration, Jolene stared at him in disbelief. The man who always purported to be a gentleman of the highest caliber let down his guard and revealed a part of his personality that caught her by surprise. His heated gaze exposed the fact that Alastair had experienced the meaning of passion. Jolene wondered whom it could have been with. Her half brother Robert had not exclusively owned the title of being a ladies' man. Had Alastair been living another life unknown to his closest friends? He always kept his affairs private.

"You're blushing," he said, smirking.

"Oh, I am?" She pulled her hand away and placed it on the side of her face, feeling the hot flesh underneath. "I guess I am."

"I have made you uncomfortable. Forgive me."

"No, I had not expected such a testimony coming from you. You are quite right. I know little about you."

"Jolene, it is not my intention by this dinner to put you under any pressure whatsoever. Please, do not feel obligated to me in any way."

She sensed the uncertainty and fear in his voice. Apparently, Alastair did not want to pressure her into more than she wanted to give. Neither did he want a broken heart, which Jolene already knew lay vulnerable underneath his shirted chest. As she thought about her own emotions, she wasn't quite sure what she wanted in regard to Alastair. She had promised Robert she would not toy with his affections but would be honest.

"I do not feel pressured," she admitted. "Nevertheless, I shall always be grateful to you for breaking Geoffrey's nose." Alastair flashed a relieved smile, and she continued. "I will admit, in my foolishness, I did not take the time to see who you truly are after my arrival. Nevertheless, I can assure you now that I am intrigued and wish to get to know you better." She lowered her eyes to her glass, carefully choosing her next words. "I promise to be honest with you regarding my emotions, but I cannot promise you…"

"Love," he answered for her. "I understand, and it should be as such. On the other hand," he paused, returning to the heated gaze he gave her earlier, "I will not deny, even now, I am hopelessly in love with you. If you are willing to at least give us a chance, I would be eternally devoted as a friend or lover."

A warmth of affection swelled in her heart for Alastair. "Give me time to find my heart again." Jolene placed her hand on her chest, hoping he would understand it only recently had been broken and needed time to heal.

"Of course," he replied with empathy.

The waiter arrived with their selections, and Jolene and Alastair chatted throughout the dinner hour about a variety of subjects. Feeling as if the weight of the world had lifted from her shoulders, she had a deep inner sense that an incredible journey of discovery lay ahead.

CHAPTER 24

The weeks passed, and Jolene spent time with Alastair during family affairs, as well as dining out and walks in the park. She learned more about him each passing day. After taking the time to turn her attention toward him wholeheartedly, Jolene discovered that she greatly enjoyed his company.

To her surprise, he showed himself to be civically informed and outspoken, with aspirations for politics that she admired. He possessed deep convictions about social injustice and hoped someday to run for office in his district. Frankly, she thought he could go all the way to Prime Minister if he put his mind to it.

As Robert and Grace's nuptials neared, so did the agonizing decision about what to do about Vienna. The lease on her own estate would expire, and the thought of going home brought mixed emotions. A part of her wanted to return to the roots that she knew and the memory of her stepfather, who left her with a title and more money than she needed. However, her real family was here, in England, with her mother and Robert. Philippe did not seem to mind, and she wondered if he would consider purchasing a home nearby rather than returning to Austria.

"You look absolutely beautiful," Suzette commented.

Jolene brought her wandering thoughts back. She reached forward and straightened the corner of Grace's veil so it would lay smoothly.

Grace's mother smiled approvingly. Jolene stood silently

watching the bride examine herself in the mirror for her last fitting. The women decided to make a day of it with lunch, shopping, and trying on the dress all rolled into one busy afternoon. Poor Grace looked exhausted but like an angel.

Her Paris seamstress, recommended by her mother, had done an outstanding job. The beautiful white dress of brocade satin and lace fit perfectly, outlining Grace's petite frame. With no further adjustments to be made, Grace begged for a reprieve.

"Two more days and I'll be married," she heaved a weary sigh. "I need to sleep, or I will swoon from exhaustion at the altar."

"You do look exhausted," Jolene agreed, "But you have a glow about you nonetheless. I'm so happy that you and Robert found one another."

"Oh, Jolene, if it weren't for you encouraging me to keep hoping, this would never have come about. We both are thankful for your matchmaking abilities."

"Well, I for one am delighted that Robert found such a wonderful woman," Suzette gushed. "You have the right temperament and gumption to keep him on the straight and narrow."

"Oh, I don't doubt that." Grace giggled. "I have him wrapped around my little finger, but adoringly, of course." She wiggled the appendage before everyone.

Grace's mother had a few more words with the seamstress, thanking her for a job well done. When she finished, Suzette and Mrs. Whitefield went to the parlor together to chat, leaving Jolene and Grace alone.

"You make a beautiful bride," Jolene repeated.

"You will too someday. I'm sure of it."

Jolene, speechless, returned a blank stare.

"How are you and Alastair getting along?" Grace asked hopefully.

"Fine, I think. I've been considering returning along with Father to Austria after you wed."

"Oh, dear," Grace moaned. "Please don't leave us."

"Well, you and Robert will be off on a two-month honeymoon holiday," Jolene protested. "There is nothing to keep me here unless…"

"Unless Alastair asks for your hand in marriage?" Grace grinned mischievously. "If he did, would you accept?"

"Now, how am I supposed to answer that question? If I say no, I'll hurt your feelings, and if I say yes, you'll run and tell him, won't you?"

Grace turned and looked at herself in the mirror, puffing her hairdo a bit after taking off the veil. Her faced looked wickedly mischievous.

"Do you know something I don't?" Jolene pressed.

"I know nothing," she said, wiping the smile off her face.

Jolene rolled her eyes. "Well, I would be surprised because your brother has been less than affectionate with me. I have never received anything more than a mere peck, and I know it is because of my affair. He despises me for it."

Grace spun around. "Really?" she drawled. "It sounds like Robert."

"What do you mean?"

"Well, frankly, I think he was so afraid of receiving a broken nose from Alastair, he didn't make any advances. I practically had to beg him for a passionate kiss."

Jolene's eye widened. "Well, that is shocking."

"Maybe that is what is wrong with Alastair. Robert has threatened him to such an extent that he isn't making any advances either."

"Well, I never actually pictured Alastair doing such a thing anyway," Jolene declared. "However, the way he spoke to me once on the subject of passion, it did make me wonder."

Grace's brows rose. "Oh, he's a good man all right, but don't let that fool you. When he and Robert were in university together, he partook of the fruit too, if you get my drift." Grace reached forward and grabbed Jolene by the arm. "Here is what I think you should do. You make the first move. Just kiss him if that's what is standing between you. See if the spark is there."

"That dangerous spark," Jolene said, chiding herself. "I don't wish to get burned."

Grace laughed. "Maybe that's exactly what you and Alastair need to move things along."

-·✳·-

"You need to kiss her passionately," Grace admonished Alastair. "Otherwise, how will she know if there is a flicker of sexual attraction between the two of you? You're acting as bad as Robert did."

"As Robert did?" His brow furrowed like a concerned father.

"It was your fault for threatening the poor man," she bemoaned. "I practically had to throw myself at him to give me a decent kiss. Thankfully, once we're married, I get all of him." She gave Alastair a sisterly poke with her index finger. "So why haven't you taken Jolene in your arms and swept her off her feet?"

"Ouch," he complained, rubbing his arm where she jabbed him. "I'm afraid she will think I'm trying to take advantage of her," he replied, frowning over the lingering pain. "What if she finds it insulting?"

Graced roared with laughter. "Insulting?"

"Well, after what happened, wouldn't a woman think that I was trying to take advantage of prior weaknesses? I do not wish to disrespect her by making her believe I'm no better than that dastardly fake viscount."

"Alastair Whitefield, do you love her or not?" She raised her voice loud enough for the servants to hear her bellow.

"Shush," he whispered, glancing about embarrassed. "Of course I do." He raked his hand through his hair in frustration. "I may come across as the gentlemanly debonair male, but I assure you that a terrible ache persists underneath my pounding heart. If I don't marry her, I'll surely go mad."

"Oh, dear, you have it bad," Grace said, grinning in delight. "I have it on good authority that she is only waiting for you to make a move. If you don't share with her the deep need in her heart, she will never reciprocate."

"Well, maybe tonight I will."

"Make it quick, because she is planning to return to Vienna with Philippe after the wedding."

"Oh, God, no," he cried.

"So you better sweep her off her feet and show her the

passion of your heart. The two of you might discover it to be an arousing occurrence." She giggled shamelessly.

"Good Lord, Grace. Robert has turned you into a little hussy." He balked.

"I know," she replied wistfully. "I do so love it."

—·✷·—

Alastair waited in the Holland parlor, pacing back and forth in worry. His sister drove him to the brink of insanity at times with all her talk about taking the initiative. When Jolene stepped through the threshold, finding him alone and ready to take her for dinner, something in Alastair's soul broke free.

Like a magnet to its attraction, his feet propelled him forward with such speed that he could barely sense what transpired. He swooped down on Jolene like a soaring eagle, scooping her up into his arms and planting a kiss on her mouth that parted her lips with his tongue. He lost control, throwing all convention of good manners to the wind.

She tasted sublime, and to his utter surprise, she moaned and fell into his arms like a helpless female begging for more. He did not care who saw them. The world disappeared into a faraway place. All that mattered was Jolene and her lips that kissed him fervently in return. If it had not been for footsteps that he heard clicking across the tiled floor outside the door, he would have continued unabashed for hours.

When he pulled away, Jolene's eyes watered with tears. Over her shoulder, he saw the butler pass by and knew then he had to seize the moment before someone else interrupted him. He dropped to one knee and grasped her hand tightly.

"Marry me, my darling Jolene. I ardently love you so deeply that I often feel I will die without you at my side. You are the air that fills my lungs, the blood that courses through my veins, the beating of my heart, and all else that makes me a man. Marry me."

Jolene's face appeared void of emotion even though her eyes continued to water. He felt her hand tremble as he squeezed it, realizing he must be crushing her fingers. When he loosened his grip, he looked at her once again, feeling as if he were pleading for his life. Would she have him?

"Oh, Alastair," she began but then paused.

He held his breath, fighting the horrible possibility this was an introduction of denial. A lump formed in his throat.

"You are such a unique man."

Alastair lowered his head afraid of what would come next.

"You are attentive, kind, gracious, and most of all forgiving."

"But…" he responded as if to help her say the next obvious word.

"There are no doubtful buts, Alastair. You have succeeded in winning my heart, and I would be thrilled to be your wife."

His head shot upward, and he looked into her eyes. "You would… you will… you mean yes?"

"Yes," she emphatically confirmed. "Now stand up and give me another one of those luscious kisses."

He sealed her acceptance with his deepest emotions afraid he would die of ecstasy.

"Uh-hum, excuse me," came a deep voice. "Shouldn't you be having dinner and not smooching in the parlor?"

Alastair recognizing Robert's voice pulled away, looking sheepishly at his friend.

"I said yes," Jolene announced.

"Yes to what?" Robert glanced over at Alastair smirking as if he knew.

"It appears that your friend will one day be your brother-in-law."

"Well, heaven help me," Robert bellowed. "Congratulations, and you didn't even ask anyone's permission!"

"Oh, dear," Alastair said. "I haven't. Not that *your* consent matters, mind you."

"You are in luck. Philippe is having a drink with Father in his study. Why don't you go take care of that now? While you are gone, I'll try to talk some sense into my sister," he joked.

"I'll be right back." Alastair spun on his heel and headed out the doorway.

"I only have one thing to ask you." Robert narrowed his eyes and looked at her somberly. "Do you love him?"

Jolene's cheeks lifted into a broad smile. "He has done an incredible job of stealing my heart. Yes, I love him very much."

"What about Vienna? You know he wants a career in politics here, not there."

"Regardless of whether this proposal had come or not, I had decided to sell the estate and move here."

"That's wonderful news."

Alastair burst into the room out of breath.

"Well, that was fast," Robert said, looking surprised.

"He wants to speak to you in the study."

"Did he agree to the marriage?" Jolene pressed anxiously.

"Not yet. He wants to talk to you."

"Oh, dear, well regardless if I have his blessing or not, I am yours." After a quick kiss on the cheek, Jolene nearly ran down the hall. She knocked on the study and entered, finding Philippe alone inside.

"Come in," he invited, looking at her earnestly.

Jolene did so and softly closed the door behind her.

"So, Mr. Whitefield has asked for your hand in marriage," he said in a flat tone. "I told him my thoughts on the matter probably didn't matter since you had a mind of your own and would make your decision."

Jolene knelt down before him and put her hand on his knee. "But I value your blessing, Father. I want you to be happy for me."

"Do you wish to give up your status in Vienna, your childhood home, and your memories there?"

"Yes."

"I see," he replied sadly.

"Do you want to go back?"

"Frankly, I'm not sure what I will do with myself once you are married."

"Those are decisions that we can make together later on. If I sell the estate in Vienna, then I can speak with Alastair about purchasing a home. There will be plenty of room for all of us," she heartedly offered.

"I wouldn't think of it," Philippe objected. "The two of you should live as husband and wife without me wandering around."

"Then I will make sure that you have whatever you need," Jolene assured him. "Does that mean I have your blessing to marry him?"

"Yes, if you truly love him, then you have my blessing. The man is enamored out of his senses with you, so I am sure he will treat you well. That is all that I care about."

Jolene leaned forward and kissed him on the cheek. "Thank you." She rose to her feet and brushed the wrinkles from her skirt. "I'm off to tell him. Oh, what an exciting time it is. Grace and Robert will wed, and then Alastair and I will set a date. I'm so happy I could squeal!"

Jolene sprinted down the hall and burst into the parlor interrupting Robert and Alastair. "I have his blessing," she cried.

"Thank goodness." Alastair pulled her into an embrace and then looked over her shoulder at Robert. "We better get you and Grace at the altar so we can make plans."

Robert's face went ashen. "Nervous?" Alastair laughed.

"Who me?" Robert said, scoffing off the inference. "Never."

CHAPTER 25

Robert stood still as the valet made a final adjustment to his tie.

"There, my lord, I believe it looks acceptable."

He glanced in the mirror and agreed that it appeared straight but also noted his petrified countenance.

"That will be all, Giles. You may go."

"May I once again wish you and Miss Whitefield great joy," he said.

"Thank you."

As he left, his father entered probably to remind him that the driver still waited downstairs to take them to St. Martin-in-the-Fields.

"My goodness, but you look quite pale," his father remarked with a smirk. "Are you feeling all right?"

"Yes. A bit nervous, I suppose."

"Brings back memories of the day I married your mother," the duke replied.

"I remember it as well, even though I was a young lad." Robert glanced at himself one more time in the mirror. "I suppose we better get on with it then. Is Mother ready?"

"More than ready."

Robert halted, remembering the gnawing question he wanted to pose before departing. He stood before his father, hoping to gain guidance.

"You have made Mother incredibly happy all these years," he said. "Do you have any advice on how I may do the same for Grace?" An appreciative smile brightened his father's face.

"For a woman, words of love are not always enough. Never stop showing your love for Grace through deed, physical affection, and the way you satisfy her intimately behind closed doors. Women are delicate creatures who need attention and reassurance of your devotion. In return, she will give you the respect that you desire from a wife."

Robert pondered his father's wise words and took them to heart. "Thank you for the guidance."

"I don't tell you often enough," he said, putting his hand upon Robert's shoulder. "But I am proud of you. When I am gone and you inherit the title and estate, I know that you will continue to bring honor to the Holland name. Hopefully, Grace will give you a son to carry on our family legacy."

"Well, a child will arrive long before you depart this world," Robert said assuredly. "I am happy in my profession while you live out the remainder of your days breeding good steeds."

"Are you coming?" His mother suddenly appeared on the threshold, gasping and out of breath. "For heaven's sake, Robert, you will be late for your wedding."

"Wouldn't want that," Robert replied. He smiled affectionately at his father and patted him on the shoulder as well. A moment later they were running down the stairs to the waiting car.

Robert glanced at his pocket watch numerous times chiding himself for taking so long. The London traffic on the way to the church did not help matters either. When they arrived, he sprinted off to meet Alastair and the vicar, who were waiting for him in an anteroom off to the right of the sanctuary. When the final guests had been seated, one of the ushers opened the door and announced everything was ready.

"You look a fright," Alastair said. "Take a deep, calming breath."

Robert's forehead beaded with sweat, and he took out his handkerchief and dabbed his forehead. "I'm a nervous wreck," he admitted.

"You'll do fine."

The vicar led the way, and Robert and Alastair took their places. When the music began, Robert noticed Alastair turn and look over his shoulder. No doubt he wanted to see Jolene, his bride-to-be, walk the aisle. Robert froze in his stance. When Jolene arrived, he quickly glanced in her direction.

The noise of the congregation rising to their feet signaled to Robert that Grace would be next. With the organ crescendo, he knew that his bride slowly made her walk on the arm of her father. He wanted to look but could not. Instead, he tightly shut his eyes and heard Alastair whisper in his ear.

"She looks like a beautiful angel."

Finally, Grace arrived. They stood side by side as her father gave her into his hand. He gazed at his future wife, who smiled at him warmly. Behind the veil, he could see tears of joy.

"Dearly beloved, we are gathered here today to join this man and woman in holy matrimony."

Robert felt as if he stood on the edge of heaven. He listened intently to every word the vicar spoke. When it came to pronouncing his vows, the anxiousness he experienced earlier gave way to peace.

"Wilt thou have this woman to be thy wedded wife, to live together after God's ordinance in the holy estate of matrimony? Wilt thou love her, comfort her, honor, and keep her in sickness and in health; and, forsaking all others, keep thee only unto her, so long as ye both shall live?"

"I will."

Proud that he had not become tongue-tied, he found it impossible not to smile as she repeated her promise in return. The words of his father kept playing over and over in his mind as she did so. "Love her not only in word but in deed…"

The exchange of rings nearly brought him to tears as he slipped it on Grace's cold finger. "With this ring I thee wed, with my body I thee worship, and with all my worldly goods I thee endow. In the name of the Father, and of the Son, and of the Holy Ghost. Amen."

As the ceremony neared conclusion, a deep peace flooded Robert's soul. He had found contentment and love with Grace.

-·⁂·-

When the service ended, Jolene stood outdoors with the other attendees throwing flower petals on Grace and Robert. Her heart swelled with happiness over their good fortune. Next to her stood a remarkable man, whom she finally allowed the opportunity to capture her heart.

She glanced over at her mother, standing arm in arm with the man she loved. Next to her, as if nothing looked out of place, stood her father. She often wondered if he still secretly loved her mother in spite of the past. Regardless, he had found happiness and contentment in his situation in life. Forgiveness had healed the family.

Everyone's attention centered on Robert and Grace, whose faces beamed with broad smiles of love and joy. They belonged to one another, and Jolene knew beyond a doubt that their years together would be happy.

Finally she turned and glanced at Alastair, smiling at his friend's good fortune. When he caught her glimpse, he slipped his arm around her waist and whispered sweetly in her ear.

"When the two of them come back from their honeymoon, it will be our turn," he proclaimed. It only seemed right that Robert would be Alastair's best man, and Grace, her maid of honor.

"Indeed," she sighed. "It will be our turn."

"Will you be happy with me?" Alastair asked as if he needed reassurance.

Jolene grinned, having no doubt in her mind that she had chosen the right man. "I know I will," she said. She gave him a quick peck on the cheek. "I love you."

Alastair's eyes sparkled hearing her declaration. She glanced at her family once again, grateful for happy endings.

The End

About the Legacy Series

The Legacy Series has been a fascinating journey as a writer. Book One in the series, *The Price of Innocence*, was my first independently published novel, which realized my dream of writing a book. It took me over eighteen months to pen, mostly because of the time I spent doing background research and questioning my sanity. Releasing it into the world turned out to be the most terrifying experience of my life. The story has been loved and hated.

The second book in the series, *The Price of Deception*, I wrote during a turbulent time in my life, which probably accounts for the turbulent story. It has been well received, and I had not planned to do Book Three until readers demanded more.

The Price of Love, the third in the series, took me a long time to write. I knew reader expectation was high because individuals became attached to the characters.

Of course, I fully intended for the series to end at Book Three, but there were a group of readers who continued to entice me to write Book Four, *The Price of Passion*.

Please, I beg you, do not ask for Book Five, as I'll be entering the years of World War I and don't wish to bring sorrow to the characters I have grown to love as well.

To all my wonderful followers who have stayed with me

throughout this series, I thank you from the bottom of my heart. Hopefully, you will continue to enjoy other stories that I have penned and new ones I will write in the future.

ABOUT THE AUTHOR

With Russian blood on my father's side and English on my mother's, I blame my ancestors for the lethal combination of my DNA that influences my stories. Tragedy and drama might be found between the pages, but I eventually give readers a happy ending.

I live in the beautiful, but rainy, Pacific Northwest. My hobby (more of an obsession) is researching my English ancestry and expanding my family tree. To keep the memory of my ancestors alive, I often use their names in my novels.

My usual genre is historical fiction with romantic elements and historical romance set in the Victorian and Edwardian eras. My books include:

The Price of Innocence (Permanently Free) – Book One of the Legacy Series

The Price of Deception – Book Two of the Legacy Series

The Price of Love – Book Three of the Legacy Series

The Price of Passion – Book Four of the Legacy Series

The Legacy Series Box Set

The Phantom of Valletta

Dark Persuasion (2012 finalist in the USA Best Book Awards for Romance)

A Portrait of Perfection (A Dark Gothic Tale of Love and Betrayal)
A Christmas Oath: Novelette
A Christmas Mission: Novelette
Ladies of Disgrace Series

I also write novellas, *Romance With a Kiss of Suspense*, under the pen name of Nora Covington. Works to date include:
Thorncroft Manor
Whitefield Hall
Blythe Court
Romance With a Kiss of Suspense Box Set
Visit my official website at http://vickihopkins.com